"Just to be clear, this is *not* a date."

Roman shrugged, shooting her a knowing smile. "If you say so. But are you sure this non-date has nothing to do with the fact that you wanted me to kiss you in the library the other day?"

Grace blinked. "When did I say that?"

He grinned. "Sweetheart, you didn't have to. It's been seven years, but I can still read you like a book."

"I seriously doubt that," she said, but her eyes told a different story. Like maybe she worried that he was right. "I'm not the same naive, trusting woman I was back then. And *don't* call me *sweetheart*."

He shrugged. "Sorry, *Gracie*. I thought you liked terms of endearment."

"But that's not why you said it. You're not nearly as charming as you think you are."

"But I *am* charming," he said, waiting for a kick in the shin.

She rolled her eyes instead. "I know you *think* so."

"Honey, I *know* so."

* * *

Back in ~~the~~ ~~Salem~~ ~~Street~~ *t of the*
Dyn

Pa
C

Dear Reader,

Writing can be a very lonely business. Working on these multiauthor continuities is a real treat.

Roman and Gracie's story was especially poignant for me, as I've been going through some huge changes and bumpy times in my own life. Writing their happy ending has given me renewed hope for my own happily-ever-after and reminded me that life has a way of working itself out. And you can never, EVER give up.

Michelle Celmer

MICHELLE CELMER

———

BACK IN THE ENEMY'S BED

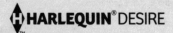

Special thanks and acknowledgment are given
to Michelle Celmer for her contribution to the
Dynasties: The Newports miniseries.

ISBN-13: 978-0-373-73497-9

Back in the Enemy's Bed

Recycling programs
for this product may
not exist in your area.

Printed in U.S.A.

www.Harlequin.com

Michelle Celmer is a bestselling author of more than thirty books. When she's not writing, she likes to spend time with her husband, kids, grandchildren and a menagerie of animals.

Michelle loves to hear from readers. Like her on Facebook or write her at PO Box 300, Clawson, MI 48017.

Books by Michelle Celmer

Harlequin Desire

The Nanny Bombshell
Princess in the Making
More Than a Convenient Bride
Demanding His Brother's Heirs
The Doctor's Baby Dare

Dynasties: The Newports

Back in the Enemy's Bed

Black Gold Billionaires

The Tycoon's Paternity Agenda
One Month with the Magnate
A Clandestine Corporate Affair
Much More Than a Mistress

The Caroselli Inheritance

Caroselli's Christmas Baby
Caroselli's Baby Chase
Caroselli's Accidental Heir

Visit the Author Profile page at Harlequin.com, or michellecelmer.com, for more titles.

For Mike and Trevor

One

Grace Winchester didn't get nervous.

As the youngest of the Winchester daughters, she may have had a privileged and pampered childhood, but as an adult she was no spoiled heiress. She'd worked damned hard building her fashion-design business, and she was a well-known and respected activist for women's rights. In a world where men dominated, she'd trained herself over the years to believe that there wasn't *anything* she couldn't do.

Okay, so there was *one* thing.

She couldn't say no to her father.

The closest thing to royalty in Chicago, Sutton Lazarus Winchester was not the sort of man who took no for an answer. One stern look from those piercing green eyes and people fell in line. But with all the recent scandal surrounding their family, and Sutton's failing health, lately she could see the worn-away edges on his harsh manner and hoped that he would take pity on her. Just this once, because what he was asking of her was truly her worst nightmare.

"Daddy, I don't want to do this."

Her father, sitting like a king on his throne at his massive teak desk, in his equally massive office in the Winchester estate, didn't even look up from the laptop screen. He'd been ill for months, sometimes barely strong enough to climb out of bed. But today was a good day. He even had some color in his hollow cheeks. "We all do things we don't want to, Princess. It's called life."

She felt herself being reduced to the whining and stubborn adolescent who would stomp her foot and huff when her parents told her no. Which honestly hadn't been all that often. She was the baby of the family, and with a bat of her ultra-long super-dark lashes most everyone gave her what she wanted. But what he was asking her to do now? When he'd said the words, they shook her deep to her core.

Roman Slater is coming to speak to me and I want you here.

Roman Slater, owner of the top private investigation firm in the Midwest, Slater Investigation Services, and the one man on the face of the planet whom Gracie swore never to speak to again. Roman

Slater, who'd swept her off her feet and promised to love her forever, then betrayed her and her family in the worst way possible. And not just once, but *two* times.

All of her life people had used Gracie to get to her father, but she'd thought Roman was different. She'd thought he'd truly loved and trusted her. And she had trusted him with not only her family, but her heart.

Big mistake.

"I don't understand why I need to be in the meeting," she told her father, and if she were hoping for an explanation, she didn't get it. Sutton Winchester never justified his demands, or explained himself. He'd never had to.

"You're staying," he said, an edge of impatience in his tone. It was the voice he used when she was pushing her luck.

The reality of the situation began to sink in. In only a few minutes Roman would be standing there, in the flesh, in her father's office. So many mixed feelings buzzed through her brain she felt dizzy and disoriented. Instinct was telling her to run and hide, and though she knew that it wasn't physically possible for her heart to sink, it sure felt as if it had. It was currently somewhere south of her spleen.

Earlier in the day, before her father summoned her home, life had been good. In fact, it had been great. Her new line of purses was flying off the shelves in every boutique in every major city in the

United States, and the new fashion app she'd recently created was now on smartphones and tablets all over the world. So other than not having any time for a personal life, and being a tiny bit lonely, she couldn't complain. Now it felt as if her world had been thrown totally off axis.

Why did it have to be her? Couldn't her sister Eve take her place? She was the CEO of the family business, Elite Industries, the multimillion-dollar real estate giant Sutton had founded. The business that Roman had recently, under the direction of Sutton's mortal enemy, Brooks Newport, tried to take down in a scandal of epic proportions.

If there was a competing royal family in Chicago, the Newport brothers, Brooks, Graham and Carson, were it. The Newport brothers were self-made millionaires with axes to grind. Brooks in particular had made it his mission to crush Sutton, run his business into the ground, and ostracize Gracie and her sisters, Nora and Eve. Which had nearly slammed the brakes on the intense love affair between Eve and Graham Newport, Gracie's future brother-in-law.

And Roman had helped him orchestrate the entire media smear campaign against their family. As if he hadn't betrayed her family enough already. Seven years after the first scandal he'd been involved with, in which the Winchesters had been exonerated of any wrongdoing, he was coming back for more. But once again Brooks's outrageous claims had no basis in reality, and in the end had only made the man look like the petty and greedy power-hungry narcissist that he was.

"After all the lies Brooks and Roman spread about us, why take a meeting with Roman at all?" Gracie asked her father. "Have you forgotten the way he dragged our family name through the mud? *Twice!* And the horrible things that they said you did this time?"

If she had been hoping for outrage, she didn't get it. In fact, Sutton didn't so much as bat an eyelash. "I haven't forgotten," he said.

Gracie adored her father, but she wasn't blind to his faults. And he had more than his fair share. He'd lived large most of his life. He was a narcissistic, arrogant, womanizing jerk, who drank, smoked and lived hard, but he would never sink so low as to commit date rape. And four of the five illegitimate children Brooks had accused him of fathering were a genetic mismatch. Carson, however, had tested positive, proving beyond a shadow of a doubt that he was Sutton's illegitimate son. Gracie and her sisters were still reeling from the news that they had a half brother. Sutton's numerous romantic affairs were no secret. But Gracie had strong suspicions that his relationship with Cynthia Newport had been more than an affair. She knew that her parents' marriage had been one based on financial compatibility more than love, but it still hurt to think that Sutton had been in love with someone other than their mother, Celeste.

But enough already. She was tired of the rumors and conjecture. Sutton was dying and Gracie just wanted him to be able to go in peace.

Not only had the scandal affected Sutton's failing health, but the risk to their company had been profound, and they were in jeopardy of losing several multimillion-dollar accounts if the attacks on Sutton's reputation didn't stop. Eve had managed to keep the company on an even keel, but now that she was pregnant with Graham's baby, things were even more complicated.

And this whole mess was thanks to Roman and what Grace considered to be his less-than-impressive PI skills. When she thought of all the pain he had caused, all the suffering and humiliation he had subjected them to, anger lit a fire in her belly.

She would choose anger over shaky nerves any day.

"What if Brooks sent him here to dig up more dirt?" she said, hoping to talk some sense into her father. "So he can finish the job and destroy our family."

Sutton folded his hands on the desk in front of him and looked up from the computer screen with the same clear green eyes she saw every morning in the mirror. For a sixty-five-year-old, he'd been in impressive physical shape until his lung cancer diagnosis earlier this year. Now his poor health was undeniable. Though he was a true fighter, the cancer had spread to his lymph nodes and there was nothing that his team of doctors could do. It was only a matter of time.

Today, thankfully, was a good day. Some days lately, he could barely make it out of bed.

"Roman didn't request to see me," Sutton said. "I asked for this meeting."

It took a second or two to process what he'd said, then her jaw nearly came unhinged, right along with her temper. And she did something that she never, *ever* did. She raised her voice to him.

"*Why* would you do that, Daddy? After all the family has been through, how could you even think of letting that man in our home?"

"It's something I need to do," he said firmly, and there was a softness in his gaze, a look of resignation in his eyes that broke Gracie's heart. Sutton never showed weakness. She had never once seen him cry, or lose his composure, and rarely had she seen him truly angry. But this look of defeat was more than she could take.

She felt her own anger, and what little was left of her resolve, fizzle away. She had to remember that her father had very limited time left on this earth. Weeks. Months. No one could say for sure. If meeting with Roman meant so much to him, what choice did she have but to respect his wishes? Her pride be damned…and her nerves, because although Gracie Winchester never got nervous, right now her heart was thumping against her kidneys and her palms had begun to sweat.

The sudden rap on the door nearly startled her right out of her Manolo Blahniks and she automatically reached up to check her hair, which she had smoothed into a tasteful chignon that morning. Suddenly she found herself wishing she'd worn it down. Though she had no clue why.

As her father's assistant opened the door, Gracie nervously smoothed the front of her Versace skirt, then folded her hands behind her back, so no one would see them trembling.

"Roman Slater to see you, sir."

Gracie felt as if the room was spinning around her. Her heart was pounding hard, and that irrational urge to run was back, but her knees were so weak she would never make it to the door.

Or out the nearest window.

"See him in," Sutton said, and Gracie stood frozen, trying not to hyperventilate.

The assistant stepped back and with a sweeping motion of her hand invited the family's worst enemy into their most sacred domain. Gracie held her breath as the bane of her existence strolled through the doorway, as though he didn't have a care in the world.

Wearing all black, he cut an impressive figure in

tailored slacks, a dress shirt unbuttoned at the neck and a sport coat that showcased his wide shoulders, thick arms and narrow hips. All designer label.

So different from the Roman of their youth, the jeans-wearing, T-shirt-sporting college student who never gave a hoot about fashion. But now, as owner of a multimillion-dollar company, he had to look the part. And he did, except maybe for the hair. His dark locks were a touch too long, and a little too rumpled, but somehow it worked.

She waited for the anger to crash over her like a suffocating wave, for the resentment to turn her blood to acid and eat its way through her veins, but she felt something so unexpected it took a minute to identify the emotion.

She felt...*relieved.*

Several years after Roman had betrayed her the first time, he'd gone missing on a military mission, and had been rumored to be dead. It had ripped her to pieces, even after the way he'd betrayed her. At the time, she would have given anything to have him back. Anything to change what had happened, because her leaving him was the reason he'd joined the military in the first place.

She'd thought that maybe if she had forgiven him and they had stayed together he would still be alive.

The guilt had eaten her up for months, until she'd heard on the news that he and several of his fellow soldiers were still alive and being held in a POW camp in the Middle East by an Al Qaeda offshoot. And most likely being subjected to unspeakable forms of torture. Though she had been weak with relief to know that he was alive, had he been dealt a fate *worse* than death? Would they torture him, then kill him anyway? The possibilities had kept her up nights, and robbed her of her appetite. She'd lost ten pounds in a week, and felt so tired and depressed she could barely do her job. So she'd stopped watching the news reports and reading updates in the papers. She'd pushed him as far from her mind as she could, though there hadn't been a day since then that she didn't think of him at least once.

Eventually Roman and his teammates had been rescued. When she knew he was alive, and safely back in the US, she'd felt a soothing sense of peace. She'd felt as if she could finally let go of the resentment. They were, in a sense, even.

Which was a horrible way to look at it. Her broken heart and sullied reputation couldn't hold a candle to his weeks of torture. She wouldn't wish that upon her worst enemy.

Which, come to think of it, he was.

Because recently Brooks, with Roman's help, had launched his campaign to destroy not only her father, but Gracie and her sisters as well, and that familiar old hatred had come oozing back like burning tar in her soul.

Yet here she was feeling relieved to see him?

What the hell was wrong with her?

"Roman," Sutton said, slowly rising from his seat to shake his adversary's hand, and Roman's hesitation to take it underscored his hostility.

"Sutton," he replied, contempt clear in his tone.

"You remember my daughter Grace," Sutton said and Gracie's heart sailed to the balls of her feet.

Roman turned and his soulful hazel eyes sliced through her like hot knives.

Roman had always been beautiful. Now he was a Greek god, with his wide jaw and broad shoulders. His nose had been broken at some point, and he had scars on his face. One started at his temple and bisected his left brow, coming dangerously close to his eye, and another jagged line ran across his forehead and disappeared under his dark hair. Some women might have been put off, but she thought it only enhanced his sex appeal.

Then she thought of how he'd gotten them, and that there were probably others she couldn't see, and felt a shaft of guilt.

"Grace," he said, his deep voice strumming her nerve endings, making something primitive and completely irrational stir in her belly.

Attraction.

Uh-uh. *No way.*

No normal, well-adjusted person would be physically attracted to someone who tried to ruin her life.

He reached over to shake her hand, and without

thinking, and purely out of habit, she took it, regretting the move instantly. But it was too late now.

He grabbed on firmly, and she gripped his much larger hand just as tightly. It was as if they both felt they had something to prove. It was almost amusing in its absurdity, and she wondered what he would do if she challenged him to an arm wrestle.

Roman's eyes taunted her. Dared her to say something snarky. Dared her to pull away first. She wouldn't give him the satisfaction.

She met his challenge, chin in the air, praying he wouldn't call her bluff...and sighing quietly with relief when, with the ghost of a smile, he finally let go.

Imagine that. Apparently even he had limits.

Roman turned to her father, exasperation and impatience oozing from his pores. He clearly was not there by choice. "So let's cut to the chase, Sutton. Why am I here?"

Sutton sat back down, his movements slow and precise to lessen the profound pain he suffered on a daily basis now, then gestured to one of the two chairs opposite his desk. "Relax. Have a seat."

One dark brow rising slightly, Roman folded his arms across that ridiculously wide chest, as if to say, *Yeah, right.* "Just tell me what you want. You said you have important information regarding a client of mine. Who?"

Gracie couldn't deny being curious herself. What was her father up to? And why hadn't he run it past her beforehand, so she didn't feel so left in the dark? Did it maybe have to do with something other than business? Something personal?

"I understand you're still looking for the natural father of Graham and Brooks Newport," Sutton said.

Unimpressed, Roman shrugged. "I am. So what?"

"I may be able to help you."

"Help me?" Roman said, with a deep and incredulous laugh. One that Gracie felt deep in her bones. "Is that some kind of joke? You've repeatedly fought me in my investigation, throwing up roadblocks every chance you could. Now you're saying you want to *help*? I don't buy it."

"I don't blame you for your hesitation, Roman, but for the sake of your clients you should listen to me. I have information that could help them."

Looking skeptical, but intrigued, Roman narrowed his eyes and said, "All right, what information?"

"I can't tell you."

One of those laughs rumbled in Roman's chest and he shook his head. "I'm finished with your games, Sutton."

"It's not a game. I can help them, but I have to speak to them directly. I've been thinking a lot about this since they came here with Carson."

"So why am *I* here?"

"I'd like to set up a meeting with them. As soon as they're both available. Together."

Gracie blinked with surprise. He wanted to invite

his mortal enemy here, into their home? And they'd actually already met once before? Had the cancer treatments begun to compromise his brain?

"Graham and Brooks aren't on the best of terms right now," Roman said. "As Graham's future father-in-law you should know that."

"I do. That's why I called you. I'm confident you can make them see reason."

Roman didn't look so confident, and Gracie had to side with him on this one. Graham's secret relationship with Gracie's sister Eve had made things very tense between the brothers. Now that Graham was going to have a child by Eve, he'd eased up on the Winchesters, but Brooks continued to pursue his vendetta against them, leading to fights between the brothers. And Brooks was trying to drag Carson into the mix by insisting he fight for what was rightfully his: a full quarter of the Winchester fortune. However, if Graham and Brooks knew Sutton was now willing to talk regarding their real father, whose identity had eluded them for years, perhaps they would put their differences aside.

"Why not tell Graham and have him pass the information on to his brother?" Roman asked. "If it's legitimate, Brooks will listen."

"No," Sutton said. "I have to do it here, in my office, with both of them."

"Why, Daddy?" Gracie hadn't meant to say that out loud and the sound of her own voice surprised her. It seemed to startle Roman, as well. He looked her way.

Sutton gazed up at her with what could only be described as tenderness, and said quietly, "It's just something I need to do."

The vulnerability in his eyes melted her. And forced her to do something she'd thought she would never have to again. Talk to Roman.

She met his icy gaze and swallowed past the lump building in her throat, struggling to find the anger and resentment she'd felt before he walked through the door. Did he have to look so hard and cold and intimidating? Maybe he'd learned that in the military. Because the Roman she knew had never looked at her like that before. She could barely remember him even raising his voice to her when they argued, which they hadn't really done all that much come to think of it. Their relationship had been pretty easy. Right up until the moment it wasn't. When she learned of how he'd betrayed her.

She had screamed at him then, and the worst part was that he never screamed back. He had only stood there looking remorseful, taking full responsibility for what he had done.

Though he had never actually said the words *I'm sorry*, his remorse had been clear on his face. And it wouldn't have made a difference if he had. There were no words to make up for his betrayal and all the hurt he caused. And if her father wanted this meeting, he was going to get it.

She could be snarky, but she knew Roman well enough to know that attitude wouldn't work. She shoved down her pride as far as it would go and tucked her tail firmly between her legs. She was doing it for Daddy.

"You know that my father isn't well. If this is something he needs to do I want to get it done. What will it take to get you to help?"

Her father touched her arm and said firmly, "Thank you, Princess. But let me handle this."

Two

Princess?

Really?

Roman resisted the urge to roll his eyes. He wasn't the least bit surprised to see Gracie pleading Sutton's case. She always had been, and always would be, a slave to her father's demands. A dedicated daddy's girl. Roman had learned that one a long time ago, the hard way. When it came to her loyalty, Sutton and her two sisters always came first.

Though it did look to Roman as though the old man didn't have much time left. The weight loss, the gray pallor. Roman had watched it happen to his own father when he was only fifteen, then five years later to his mother. Roman could see that Sut-

ton Winchester was knocking on death's door, and
didn't doubt that the man's excessive lifestyle had ul-
timately been his undoing. The skirt chasing, heavy
drinking and high-stress business dealings had taken
their toll.

Which was why Roman didn't feel a bit sorry for
him.

Sutton turned to Roman and asked, "Will you
arrange it?"

Yeah, right. Who the hell did Sutton think he
was, asking *anything* from Roman? He didn't owe
the man a damned thing. "Um…no. I won't."

"I'll pay you," Sutton said, and Roman's hack-
les went up.

The idea of taking the old man's money made
him sick to his stomach. He shook his head and said,
"Not gonna happen."

"What do you want? Just name it."

He opened his mouth to tell the old geezer that he
had nothing to offer that Roman could possibly want,
when something stopped him. He glanced over at
Gracie, who was doing her best not to look at Roman.
He remembered all the times in the past that Sutton
had tried to sabotage Roman's relationship with Gracie, because he never considered Roman—a military
brat—good enough for his precious daughter. But
Roman had come a long way since then. Now Sutton needed him, and clearly he had nothing to lose.

He glanced over at Gracie, casually eyeing her

up and down. "How about an hour alone with your daughter."

Gracie blinked, then blinked again, and asked in an incredulous tone, "To do *what*, exactly?"

He let a slow smile curl his lips. "Whatever I want."

She opened her mouth to speak but nothing came out. He had rendered the great Grace Winchester speechless. That was a first. And it gave him more satisfaction than he'd ever imagined it could.

"It was a joke," Roman said. "I just want to talk."

"But I don't want to talk to you," she replied, glancing nervously toward her father. Would Sutton really do that to her? Knowing Roman and Gracie's complicated past, would he really force her to speak with him?

"I'll give you fifteen minutes with her," Sutton said, cementing in Roman's mind what a bastard the man really was, selling out his own daughter.

Gracie gasped and said, "Daddy!"

She looked to Roman with pleading eyes.

"Forty-five," Roman said, ignoring her.

"Twenty," Sutton countered without missing a beat.

Un-freaking-believable.

Grace just stood there, her mouth hanging open, as if she couldn't believe this exchange was really happening. That she was being bartered like property.

"Thirty and not a minute less," Roman told Sutton. "And that's my final offer. Otherwise, you're on your own, old man."

Knowing how vain Sutton was, the "old man" comment had to stick in his craw, but he never let it show. He considered it for less than ten seconds before he said, "We have a deal."

Wow, the man truly had no scruples or decency. Gracie had offered to help, but considering her wide-eyed stare, Roman doubted this was what she had in mind. The question was, would she really do it?

Maybe Sutton had no scruples, but Roman did. "What do you say, Grace? Thirty minutes to catch up?"

Roman could see that she wanted to say no. But Sutton broke into a coughing spasm that paled his skin and stole his breath, and Grace winced.

She laid a hand on her father's shoulder until the spasm ceased then said gently, "Of course I'll do it."

"I'll see what I can do," Roman said. "But I can't promise that Graham and Brooks will cooperate."

"If anyone can get them to agree, you can," Sutton said.

An actual compliment? Wonders never ceased.

Roman turned to Grace and grinned, and the patience and compassion she showed her father evaporated before his eyes. He could feel the tension and her hatred for him radiating from every pore. And he deserved it for his boorish behavior, but if this was the only way to get Gracie to talk to him, so be it.

"When would you like your thirty minutes?" she said through clenched teeth.

"Right now works for me," he said with a grin, feeling smug about the whole situation. He hadn't been looking forward to his meeting with Sutton and had originally told him no. It had taken some convincing to change his mind and now he was glad he had. And if Sutton thought that having his daughter there would soften Roman up, he was wrong.

Well, maybe not *totally* wrong.

He had half suspected the old man would pull something like this, but when Roman saw Gracie standing there in her father's office it was still a shock.

"We can talk in the library," Gracie said stiffly, her back ramrod straight as she spun around and led him out of the room, her entire being vibrating with anger and hatred for him.

Considering what her family had been through recently, who could blame her? But she had it all wrong this time. And she owed him a chance to explain his role in the recent scandal involving her family. How it was not his intention, or even his fault, that her family was caught up in scandal.

Not this time anyway.

Her spiked heels clicked against the marble floor as she led him to the library, where they used to spend many a Sunday morning stretched out on the sofa in the sunshine, their bodies intertwined, reading the paper. Back when they were dating, of course, when she was in college and still lived at her father's estate. Roman had been fresh out of college and working his first job as a fledgling private investigator, quickly moving up the ranks of the firm.

But he had been too smug and gung ho for his own good and consequently had made the biggest mistake of his life. He'd begun investigating officials and politicians with suspected ties to the mob and Sutton's name had come up. Gracie, who had been interning at Elite Industries at the time, was implicated in making some computer files disappear and helping Sutton launder money. Roman had confronted her and she'd sworn that it wasn't true, that her father would never work with the mob and she certainly wouldn't do anything illegal. He had wanted to believe her, but he was young and stupid and the evidence had looked so overwhelming that he hadn't trusted her. By the time he had realized his mistake, it was too late.

And he'd paid for it.

The pain and anguish in her eyes as she'd berated him for his betrayal were almost more than he could take. And he had deserved each and every harsh word. He would have done anything to take it back. To go back in time and relive the past. But knowing she would never forgive him, that he didn't even deserve her forgiveness, Roman hadn't even tried to apologize. He'd ruined his career and made more than a few enemies in the mob. For his own safety he'd had to leave town.

After denying his military roots for so long, and with nowhere else to go, he'd joined the army and started a new life for himself. Started over. But his capture, and torture, and resulting PTSD, had brought to a close that phase of his life, as well.

Once again he had pulled himself up and started over, never accepting for a second that he would be anything but successful. His former training in black ops and status as a war hero had brought in the business at first, but his impeccable performance and record of success in solving cases had kept the customers calling. The firm had grown to proportions and experienced a level of success that even he hadn't imagined.

And this time, when it came to Gracie and her family, he'd done nothing wrong. He'd been doing his job, and doing it well.

Gracie ushered him into the library and shut the doors behind them. It looked just as it had seven years ago. In fact, nothing of the Winchester estate that he'd seen so far today had changed at all.

Roman strolled to the huge bay window that looked out over the grounds. Mostly bare trees swung testily in the cool wind blowing off the lake, their colorful leaves fluttering to the lawn, where workers hurried to gather them up.

"So what is this all about?" Gracie asked from

behind him. He turned to her and she did not look happy. And her mood wasn't likely to improve.

"As I said, I just want to talk."

She folded her arms and glared at him. "What if I don't want to talk to you?"

Didn't seem like she had much of a choice. He slowly and deliberately crossed the room to where she stood, his eyes never leaving her face, and stopped in front of her at a distance that was probably just a bit too close for her comfort. So that she had to look up to meet his eye. Even in her gargantuan heels.

"Sweetheart, all you have to do is listen."

It took a lot to make Grace Winchester squirm, but he was sure he had her panties in a twist right now, but she held her ground. Her confidence and competence had fascinated Roman from the day they were introduced by a mutual friend in college. She had been young and pretty, sharp as a whip, ridiculously smart and motivated, and he had been instantly drawn to her. The first time he talked to her, he could see that she felt it too—that tug.

He had always been a practical, logical person, but there had been nothing logical about his feelings for this woman he had barely known at the time. She had turned his whole world upside down. Back then she was confident, driven and full of energy. And he'd wanted her. Badly. He'd had no idea who she was until weeks later when, scanning the society pages, he happened to see a photo of Gracie and her sisters with Sutton taken at some charity event. Being a navy brat, he'd lived in bases all over the world. He'd had no clue about high-society Chicago.

He and Gracie had grown pretty close by then, and knowing she'd held that back from him had hurt his feelings and had him questioning their friendship. He'd confronted her, and her explanation for the deception had broken his heart. She'd shrugged, as if it was no big deal, and said, "People use me to get to my father all the time. When someone shows interest in me, I have a process. I had to know if you were really who you said you were."

"And you think I am?" he'd asked, hoping she'd say yes.

She'd smiled and said, "Yeah, I do. Thanks for being a *real* friend."

In that instant, he'd realized he could never be with her. He'd wanted to. More than she ever could have imagined. But friendship was the only thing she'd really needed from him. Someone to always have her back, and help keep away those people who would try to take advantage of her. And it had been shocking to see just how many there were. That's when he genuinely understood her caution, and the realization had cemented them firmly in the friendship zone. If they were to get into a romantic situation that didn't work out, he knew it would end their friendship. Then who would watch out for her? Who would be her "true" friend?

It wasn't a chance he had been willing to take. Not then anyway. But later, after he graduated, things changed. And by then it was too late to change back.

"I want to explain what happened," he told her.

Her voice ice-cold, she said, "You mean how you tried to destroy my family. *Again*."

It was the "again" that got him, and the hint of pain layered just beneath the anger in her voice. The last thing he'd wanted to do was hurt her. "Brooks hired me to investigate and I was doing my job."

She huffed. "Sure you were. By making up lies and spreading rumors about us. Just like the last time. I know my father isn't perfect, but to accuse him of date rape?"

"That wasn't me. I had no intention of accusing him of anything until I had the facts. But Brooks was pushing me for an update so I told him what information I already had. I told him that it was unsubstantiated, and I needed more time to investigate. Brooks didn't want to wait. I was just as shocked as everyone else when he went public."

Roman hadn't known that Brooks had been planning to take all that unverified evidence to the local media until it was too late. Unfortunately his brother Graham hadn't realized either that Brooks's only goal had been to take Sutton and his family down, even if his allegations were based on rumors and lies. But by then there was nothing Roman or anyone else could do to stem the flow of speculation and accusations. The damage was already done.

Definitely not Roman's fault.

"It's not as if you have a history with this sort of thing," Gracie said, her tone dripping with resentment as she propped her hands on her very sexy hips, lifted her chin high and met his gaze. As if to say, *Here I am. Take your best shot.*

"I've made terrible mistakes," he told her, and his candor made her blink with surprise. But he believed in taking responsibility for his actions, no matter how hard it might be. "I know I've caused you and your family unspeakable pain. And I've had to live with that. But I swear to you that I didn't have any knowledge of Brooks's plan and had nothing to do with it. I was just doing my job."

"Give me *one* good reason why I should believe you."

"I don't have one." If he were her, he probably wouldn't believe him, either.

She didn't seem to know what to say, when in the past she'd always had strong opinions about pretty much everything.

"Now I want to ask you a question," he said.

She shook her head. "Nope. That was not part of the deal. I'm only supposed to listen, remember? It's just like you to go back on your word."

A direct hit. Clearly she was giving him no slack. That was more like the Gracie he knew.

"Answer it, don't answer it, that's up to you," he said. "I just want to know why you let Sutton do that to you."

Her brow wrinkled with confusion, and her curiosity won out over her stubborn nature. "Do what?"

"Belittle and disrespect you."

She instantly went on the defensive, looking outraged by his accusation. "He didn't. He loves me."

"You're so used to it you don't even see it," he said, shaking his head sadly. Sutton was a textbook sociopath. Roman wasn't sure if he was even capable of genuine love. He was too narcissistic.

"See what?" she snapped.

"Let's put it this way. You have a name and it isn't *Princess*."

Gracie rolled her eyes in exasperation. "It's a term of endearment. Not an insult."

"Not during a business meeting," Roman said, and she felt her resolve falter. Okay, so it did annoy her a little when her father called her *Princess* in certain situations. Especially in business meetings. But that was just his way.

"And that's not half as bad as the way he just bartered you like property to get what he wanted," Roman said.

Ouch. He hit a raw nerve with that comment, and

it took everything in her not to wince. He was right. What her father had done to her today was beyond humiliating. And inexcusable. But she didn't believe he was intentionally disrespecting her. He was just used to getting what he wanted.

And how does that make it okay? an annoying little inner voice asked.

Simple. It didn't. There was nothing okay about the way he'd treated her, so why *did* she put up with it? He would have never done such a thing to Gracie's sisters. But then again, they wouldn't have tolerated it. Had she been so enamored, such a devoted daddy's girl, that she let him walk all over her? That he took advantage of her devotion?

The idea made her sick to her stomach.

She could blame it on his illness but she would only be lying to herself.

"No one deserves to be disrespected that way," Roman said, and she recognized his tone. She'd heard it a lot near the end of their relationship. He was *angry*. But not *at* her.

He was angry *for* her.

She had no idea what that meant, or how she should take it. Or even what she should say in response. *Thank you? Mind your own business?*

After all this time why did he even care anymore? Was this some sort of trick or manipulation? Was he using her to get to her father again?

"You should have told us *both* to go to hell," he

said, sounding genuinely mad. And he was right, she should have, so why hadn't she? Why had she...

Her thoughts came to a screeching halt.

Wait a minute. *Roman* had been the one to suggest the bargain in the first place. Was that not disrespectful, as well? Who was he to judge her father? Or her.

Her temper flared and her blood simmered in her veins. "Could you be more of a hypocrite? Are you forgetting that *you* started it? *You* put me in the hot seat."

"I did," he admitted, looking unapologetic. "And it was wrong. Absolutely. But I honestly didn't think he would do it. I thought he would throw me out on my ass. I would have if it was my daughter."

Ouch, another direct hit. Damn him. And he was right. If she were ever to have a child, she could not even imagine putting him or her in such a compromising position. "So why didn't you just walk away? You didn't want to help him in the first place so I'm sure it would have given you a lot of satisfaction to leave him hanging."

"It would," he agreed. "But it gives me *more* satisfaction to know that I talked to you, and you listened. That was all I wanted."

"Why?" she said, then immediately regretted the question. Maybe she didn't want to know why. Because the look in his eyes...

It was the one he always got right before he kissed

her. And they were standing so close that if he wanted to, he would barely have to lean forward...

"On second thought I don't want to know," she said, taking a small step back, hoping he wouldn't notice. But of course he did.

His eyes sparked with mischief. "Are you afraid you might like what I have to say? Or are you just afraid of me in general?"

Pretty much all of the above. She didn't even want to go there, but as he stepped a little closer, invading her personal space, her feet felt glued to the floor.

"I have no reason to be afraid of you," she said, cursing the slight wobble in her voice.

"I came here at your father's request for one reason, and one reason only," he told her, leaning in just a little, and she braced herself for what she already knew was coming. "Because I thought I might see you."

Damn, that was what she was afraid of.

His wry grin said he was having too much fun torturing her. And it *was* torture to be so close to him and not be able to put her hands on him. How had this happened when a few minutes ago she hated him? Well, maybe not hated. That was a very strong word. And for all their troubles, sexual attraction had never been one of them. Not even at the end.

Obviously, not even now.

The first year they'd known each other their relationship had been deeply rooted in the "just friends" category. And he truly had been her best friend. However, that had never doused the fires of a heart-melting crush. But he'd never shown an interest in her physically, so she had been convinced she wasn't his type. Until one night after a horror-movie marathon, as they were hugging goodbye at his apartment door. She had pushed up on her toes to kiss Roman's cheek, and he had leaned forwrad in that exact second to kiss hers. She had tilted one way, and he the opposite, and somehow their lips had collided.

And oh. My. God.

The kiss had gone from zero to sixty in an instant. Roman had groaned and tangled his fingers in her hair, pulled her close. Then they couldn't stop kissing, and before she knew what was happening she was off her feet. He carried her to his bedroom, where they ripped at each other's clothes, falling into a tangle on the unmade bed. The sex was even better than she had imagined it would be. And boy, had she imagined it a lot. He had more than exceeded her expectations.

They'd made love half the night, and fallen asleep in each other's arms. She'd been sure the next morning the disappointment would come. He would blame it on the bottle of wine they had shared, and ask her if they could go back to just being friends. And she'd known it would break her heart, and seeing him with another woman would destroy her, but she couldn't imagine losing his friendship.

But he had told her he loved her instead. That he had *always* loved her, and wanted her, and she'd nearly wept with relief. After that they'd been inseparable. She'd loved him with all of her heart.

Then he had betrayed her.

Three

Those warm fuzzy memories from their past turned to ice in her veins. Was he here not really to explain, but to turn her against her own father? His weapon this time wasn't lies and accusations. This time it was truth. And the truth did hurt. A lot.

But why should she trust anything he said to her?

Something in Roman's expression changed. "Did someone open a window? It just got chilly in here."

"I see what you're doing," she said, backing away from him. "You're trying to turn me against my father."

A shadow passed across his face and the temperature dropped another ten degrees. "Is that really what you think?"

She had offended him. Well, tough. "You've tried it before."

"As someone who lost both of his parents at a very young age, I would never intentionally put a wedge between a parent and a child."

"You told me my father was working with the mob! How did you think I would feel?"

"I said that I *suspected* he was. And I only told you that to keep you safe. And you didn't believe me anyway."

"And I was right. There were no mob ties, were there?"

He shook his head. "No."

"And I wasn't laundering money for him, either. Or destroying evidence. Was I?"

That made him wince a little. "No, you weren't."

"After all this time I still can't believe you would accuse me of that," she said. "I thought you knew me better."

"I didn't accuse. I asked."

"You suspected, and that was just as bad. The idea that you believed I might be capable—" Emotion rushed up to block her airway, making it impossible to finish her sentence. It was taking all her strength to hold back the sob that was working its way up.

She would not cry. He wasn't worth it.

She thought she'd put all of these feelings to rest, but here she was raw and bleeding again.

She was *not* going to cry.

"I made a mistake," he said, "and not a day has gone by since then that I haven't regretted it."

He was making it worse, being so reasonable. Admitting he was wrong. And if she didn't get a grip, she was going to go all girly on him. She was not a crier. The last time she remembered shedding a tear was the day of Sutton's cancer diagnosis. But here she was fighting back a waterfall.

He needed to go now.

"Your time is up," she said, not even looking to the clock to see if thirty minutes had passed. Or was it supposed to be twenty? She couldn't even remember. She just wanted him gone. And she hated herself for letting him get to her. For letting herself care at all. She was stronger than that. And smarter. "You have to leave."

He didn't look at his watch as he nodded. Apparently he had said all he came to say. "I'll let myself out."

Maybe he could see that she was hanging on by a very thin thread and was kind enough to spare her dignity.

She watched him cross the room to the door, noting a slight catch in his gait, as though he was favoring his left leg. He stopped on the threshold, his broad shoulders nearly filling the frame, and turned back to her. She held her breath, waiting, feeling an overwhelming sense of anticipation.

"Seven years ago, I thought I could keep the nature of my investigation from you. That alone was wrong. And when you did find out I should have trusted you when you said you weren't involved. But I was young and arrogant and I screwed up. I know I never apologized for what I did, but only because I didn't think you would ever accept it, or that I even deserved your forgiveness. But I'm saying it now. I'm sorry, Gracie."

Her heart melted. She wanted to run across the room, throw her arms around his neck and tell him that she forgave him, that she would *always* forgive him, but she had to keep her head on straight. She was caught up in the moment, in his tender honesty, and knew she would regret letting him off too easy. Besides, she didn't even know if she *did* forgive him, or if she believed he had nothing to do with the latest scandal. She didn't know what to think, so she chose her words carefully.

"I appreciate that," she said, which got her a wry, slightly crooked grin.

"I get it," he said. "You'll accept my apology in your own good time. I understand, and I'm in no hurry."

She had no idea what to say, but it didn't matter because he turned and then he was gone.

Feeling relieved, grateful, and painfully disappointed for some silly and irrational reason, Gracie collapsed into a leather chair and exhaled deeply, waiting for the flood, giving herself permission to cry. To sob her heart out if that was what she needed. But the damned tears wouldn't come.

What the heck was wrong with her?

She didn't feel sad, or hurt, or even angry with him. She wasn't sure *what* she was feeling right now, other than confused.

She had anticipated this day for seven years, and it had gone absolutely nothing like she'd imagined. She'd always envisioned him being cocky and unapologetic. Someone she would love to hate, and keep on hating. But this?

This was way worse than the anger. Or the nerves.

She thought about what Roman had said, about her father disrespecting her. And she hated how right he was. And hated herself even more for letting Sutton do it to her. For turning a blind eye for so long. She deserved his respect. She had *earned* it. But maybe he didn't even realize the way the things he did affected her. And instead of walking around with a big chip on her shoulder, she could just tell Sutton how she felt. Maybe he would apologize and promise not to do it again. It would be an amazing gift, because the great Sutton Winchester did not apologize for anything. Ever. But in his fragile condition did she want to risk upsetting him, or possibly putting a wedge in their relationship? He had so little time left.

No, she had to say something. If he passed away tomorrow she would spend the rest of her life feeling this unresolved resentment. That wasn't what she wanted.

Rising from the chair, she smoothed the front of her skirt, took a deep breath and walked back to her father's office. She rapped on the partially open door and peeked inside. Sutton was still sitting at his desk. He looked pale and exhausted. He should be in bed resting, but it was just like him to push himself to the limits and tire himself out.

She rapped softly on the door again. "Daddy, can I have a word with you?"

"What is it?" he snapped, not even looking at her.

She winced a little. That wasn't a good sign. He'd been going through some severe mood swings lately. Most likely a result of the cancer now growing in his brain. "I wanted to talk to you about what happened with Roman."

His eyes never left the screen, as if she wasn't even worth his time, and it hurt. A lot.

"What about it?" he said.

As her hands began to tremble, she realized that this was going to be harder than she'd anticipated. But she pulled herself up by her bootstraps, raised her chin and said in a semistrong yet slightly shaky voice, "It was wrong what you did."

In her life she couldn't recall ever telling him he was wrong about anything, and he clearly didn't like it.

The savvy and ruthless businessman looked up at her with eyes as cold as icicles. "And what did I do?"

The question was, what had *she* just done? He was obviously not feeling well. He looked so pale. Maybe she should have just kept her mouth shut.

Her voice trembling a little, she said, "I didn't want to talk to Roman and you shouldn't have forced me."

"We all make sacrifices, Princess."

Sacrifices? Shouldn't that have been *her* choice? "You didn't even ask me if it was okay. It was disrespectful and cruel."

He muttered a curse under his breath. He was mad at her, and she felt herself backing down again the way she always did. "I've had a long day and I'm tired." He sighed. "I don't have time for this nonsense."

He thought her feelings were nonsense? Was that seriously how he felt about her?

He's not well, she reminded herself, holding her tongue. He was dying. Wasting away. For a man like Sutton, to lose his faculties had to be the highest form of humiliation.

So what was his excuse for the other twenty-six years before his diagnosis? that annoying little voice asked. But after what she had been through with Roman today, she didn't have the energy or the will to make it an issue. If it weren't for the pile of designs on her drawing table at the office, she would go home, crawl into bed, hide under the covers and stay there until her dignity returned. But that just wasn't her. She was a fighter.

"I'll leave you alone," she said, backing away from his desk.

"I'm not through with you yet," he said testily, stopping her in her tracks. Then he closed his eyes and rubbed his temples, and she wondered if it really was either the cancer in his brain or the treatments making him so temperamental.

She swallowed her pride and in the calmest voice she could manage, said, "Yes?"

"I need you to do something for me." He gazed up at her and the softness was back in his eyes. "Please."

It was the *please* that got her. That melted her into a puddle. And every bit of resolve went out the window that she herself had wanted to jump through earlier. "Of course. Anything."

"I need you to start seeing Roman again."

It took a second for the meaning of his words to settle in, and when they did her jaw nearly hit the desk. There was no way he meant what she thought he meant. After what she had just said to him? "Seeing him where?"

"You're going to date him." It was a demand, not a request, and she was so stunned, she couldn't form a reply. Now Sutton was pimping her out?

Finally she managed, "Wh-what if he doesn't want to see me?"

"He's clearly still attracted to you, and I need to know what he's up to."

Still attracted to her? Oh no he didn't. He did not just suggest…

Sutton glanced up at her and did a double take. She must have looked as horrified as she felt.

"I'm not asking you to *sleep* with him," he said, though his tone suggested he would have expected her to do it had he asked.

Or maybe she was being overly touchy under the circumstances. He wasn't necessarily in his right mind.

"Just take him out a few times. You used to be good friends. He'll open up to you," Sutton said.

What did he think she was, a spy or something? A female James Bond?

She couldn't deny the lure of spending time with Roman. Purely out of curiosity, of course. Just to see what he was like now, and how much he had changed. But this was crazy. "Daddy, I don't know if I can do that. You know I'm not a good liar."

"So don't lie," he said, and when she frowned his gaze softened. "Princess, I don't have much time left and I don't want to spend it embroiled in another scandal. Brooks is still determined to take us down and I think Roman is helping him."

"He said he's not."

Her father's brows lifted. "And you trust him?"

She sighed. Of course not. What reason would she have to? He'd lied to her before. Why would she assume that he would be honest about anything? She was smarter than that.

She shook her head. "No, I don't."

He held his hand out and she took it. His skin felt papery thin and so cold. He had aged so much in the past few months, and it broke her heart.

He squeezed. "I need to know what to expect, Princess. You're the only one I trust. I need you to do this for me."

And the guilt train pulled into the station. This was how he got her every time, and as much as she wanted to, as always she couldn't say no.

"Okay," she told him. "I'll do it."

"Do you have a date for the Welcome Home fund-raiser this weekend?"

She rarely took dates to charity functions, but a social interlude in a very public place sounded like a good idea. Though Roman had always hated formal affairs, and having to wear a "monkey suit." But Welcome Home was an organization to assist wounded vets and their families, and being a wounded vet himself, he might make an exception.

"I'll ask him to join me," she said, then added, "but only as a friend. I will not lie to him, or lead him on in any way. And if he says no, I'm done. I won't beg him."

"Trust me, Princess," he said, with that rare tenderness in his eyes. "He isn't going to say no."

How in the hell had he ended up here?

Roman sat in the back of the limo, watching the

lights of Chicago whiz by through the tinted window, but the view inside the vehicle was the one getting him all hot and bothered.

Gracie was seated opposite him, with one tanned, shapely leg peeking out from the slit of an apricot silk evening gown. She was on her cell phone, speaking fluent French. She'd always had great legs, but they hadn't come from hours of working out in the gym. She was one of those naturally thin women who could eat whatever they wanted and whom other women loved to hate.

Roman wasn't fluent in French, but he knew enough to understand that it was a business call. After several minutes she said goodbye and slid her phone into her clutch.

"Sorry about that," she said.

"That's okay," he told her, lowering his gaze to the leg playing peekaboo with her gown. "I've just been sitting here enjoying the view."

She shot him a look dripping with exasperation. *"Really."*

He grinned and gestured out the tinted window. "The view of the city," he said, though she knew damn well what he was really looking at. And he couldn't help but notice that she made no attempt to cover her leg.

She *liked* that he was looking. And he liked that she liked it. Clearly the past seven years had done nothing to douse his desire for her. The musky scent of her perfume enveloped him like a warm blanket, heating him to the core. It was the same brand she'd always worn. Her silky hair, pulled up in a mass of blond curls, revealed a long, slender neck he would love to kiss, and diamond-studded ears he was dying to nibble on. As a young woman she'd been cute and spunky with a mischievous glint in her eyes. Now, at twenty-seven, she was a knockout. And despite all the time that had passed, and all the discord between them, he still felt a familiarity and a closeness that puzzled him.

"So, are you ready to tell me what all this is about?" he asked her.

"All what?" she asked innocently, but he could see her squirm a little. She had always been a terrible liar. Which made what he'd put her through seven years ago even worse. Though she had never given him a reason not to, he hadn't trusted her, and he'd paid the price.

"Tonight," he said. "Your text was very…elusive. I was surprised when I got it."

"I was a little surprised that I sent it."

"Didn't get enough of me the other day, huh?" he asked with a grin, which seemed to make her even more uncomfortable. "Or you just couldn't get a date."

"Just to be clear, this is *not* a date. This is two acquaintances sharing a ride to a social function. And as I already explained, since it's a fund-raiser for wounded vets, I thought you would be interested in attending."

He shrugged, shooting her a knowing smile. "If you say so."

"Some of the most influential people in the state will be there. You'll make good connections."

"You sure this nondate has nothing to do with the fact that you wanted me to kiss you in the library the other day?"

She blinked. "When did I say that?"

He grinned. "Sweetheart, you didn't have to. It's been seven years, but I can still read you like a book."

"I seriously doubt that," she said, but her eyes told a different story. Like maybe she worried that he was right. "I'm not the same naive, trusting woman I was back then. And *don't* call me *sweetheart*."

"How about Princess? Can I call you that?"

She glared at him.

He shrugged. "Sorry, *Gracie*. I thought you liked terms of endearment."

"But that's not why you said it. You're not nearly as charming as you think you are."

"But I *am* charming," he said, waiting for a kick in the shin.

She rolled her eyes instead. "I know you *think* so."

"Honey, I *know* so."

She let the *honey* comment go. "Funny, but I don't recall you being this arrogant."

He grinned. "And you're as stubborn as you ever were. Just like my sister."

"How is April? I seem to remember that she was getting married."

Yeah, and Gracie was supposed to be his date, but he'd screwed that up. "She's living in California with her husband, Rick, and their twin boys, Aaron and Adam."

Gracie softened into that gooey-eyed look that women got whenever children were mentioned. "Oh my gosh! Twins?"

"Yep. She has her hands full."

"How old?"

"They'll be a year on Christmas Day," he said, hearing the pride in his own voice. He'd never imagined himself ever having children, so he spoiled his nephews any chance he got. He had held them both just minutes after their birth, so there was a close connection. He would lay down his life for them. And for April—not that she needed his protection. She was one of the most competent women he'd ever known.

"I was in town visiting for the holidays when she had them. Her husband was deployed at the time so I went through the entire labor with her. It gave me a whole new respect for mothers."

"Do you see them very often?"

"We Skype weekly."

"She was always such a great person," Gracie said with genuine affection in her voice.

Four years his junior, it had been exceptionally difficult for his sister when they lost their parents. And even harder for him to be away at college while she grieved alone, though she'd been taken in by a close family friend. He'd considered dropping out of school until she finished high school, but she wouldn't let him. She did visit him often, though, and she had taken to Gracie instantly. They were only a year apart in age and were both strong, capable women, though they couldn't have been any more different in their interests. April was a rough-and-tumble tomboy capable of drinking any man under the table, and she chose the armed services over college, marrying young. Gracie hadn't been interested in marriage—at least not until she finished school—and they had never really talked about a family. He wondered now if she had ever considered it. Her ambition to be a fashion designer had always been her main focus. From what he'd seen in the media, she was a raging success, and her philanthropy was legendary.

"Is she still in the navy?" Gracie asked him.

"She and her husband both," he said. "They're both stateside right now, but tomorrow, who knows?"

"It must have been difficult for her when you were a POW."

"It was." At the mere mention of his capture that

familiar sense of dread worked its way up from some-place deep inside him. But he instantly shoved it back down. It had taken intense rehabilitation to heal the physical trauma of his ordeal, and even longer to con-quer the PTSD that had tortured his soul. To this day he still suffered nightmares, and occasionally woke in a panic, drenched in a cold sweat, his mind convinced he was still in the Middle East. But he was back to being a fairly centered and functioning human being. Giving in to his demons had never been an option, and he'd fought like hell to be well again.

Though he was usually pretty good at hiding his emotions, and burying the anguish, Gracie's pained look said that after all these years, she could read him just as well as he'd read her.

For several seconds she was quiet, her eyes locked on his, then asked softly, "What was it like?"

The question threw him for a second. Aside from group therapy, and private sessions with his ther-apist, Roman had never spoken of his experience as a POW. Not even with his sister. No one ever asked. The physical scars pretty much spoke for themselves.

But despite their rocky past, he knew Gracie would never judge, or question his fortitude or brav-ery. He wasn't sure how he knew, but he just did, that despite everything that had happened between them, she genuinely cared.

So he talked.

Four

"The first few months after my rescue were almost unbearable," Roman told her. "I couldn't stop thinking about the men who didn't make it out alive. The ones who were killed in front of me, in cold blood. The survivor guilt was worse than the actual torture. I would have given my life for any one of those men. The scars will never go away, but I've made peace with myself. It wasn't easy, though."

She gazed over at him, her eyes filled with pain and regret. "I used to feel as though, because of everything that happened between us, if it hadn't been for me, you would have never joined the military in the first place. Like, maybe if I wasn't so hard on you...if I could have forgiven you..." She shrugged. "It doesn't make a whole lot of sense, I know."

The idea that she felt guilt over his leaving both surprised and disturbed him. "Gracie, my joining up had nothing to do with you. I screwed up. I was arrogant and cocky and I messed with the wrong people. Even if you had forgiven me I wouldn't have stayed because then your life would have been in danger, too. Besides, the military is in my blood. I fought it for a long time, but it's where I was meant to be."

What she didn't realize was that if it hadn't been for her, he may not have even survived the torture. Picturing her face, believing that if he endured he might see her again, had given him a reason to live as he watched his fellow soldiers die, picked off one by one as the rest had been forced to watch. One of those men had been his closest friend. A husband and father of three. To this day Roman would still give anything to switch places with him. But all he could do now was make sure that the man's family was taken care of financially. He'd set up a trust for them in their father's name. Even that hadn't assuaged the guilt, but it made it easier to live with the pain.

He leaned forward, closing the gap between them, and took Gracie's hand. It was so small and delicate compared to his own. And she didn't even try to pull away. "Trust me when I say you were better off staying away from me. And you hold no responsibility for my mistakes. I was the one who turned my back on you. I didn't trust you. I was young and stupid and arrogant. It was my fault."

The limo pulled up to the Metropol hotel where the fund-raiser was being held but she didn't let go of his hand or break eye contact. The driver steered the car into the parking structure to the VIP entrance underground. When they stopped, an attendant opened the door but Gracie just sat there looking at Roman, then she squeezed his hand.

"Roman, when I heard the false reports that you were killed, I thought I couldn't feel any worse. Then I learned of your capture, and the torture..." She paused and took a deep breath. "I know that it was nothing compared to what you were going through, but I want you to know that I thought about you and prayed for you every day."

Deep down he knew that. Maybe that was why he still felt such a strong bond to her. "Gracie, that means more to me than you could ever know."

Gracie had helped plan more charity functions than she could count, and she had to admit that the Welcome Home decorating committee had seriously outdone themselves this time. Red, white and blue tulle swirled tastefully overhead, garnished with American flag balloons and crepe streamers. The tables had been draped in white linen with blue cloth napkins and red rose centerpieces. The decor screamed patriotism and valor. And in the center of it all against the back wall a slideshow of the wounded warriors and their families the foundation had assisted played on a huge screen.

The crowd was a who's who of Chicago, with a handful of Hollywood personalities mixed in. From where she stood she could see Roman mingling with the other guests. He looked damned fine in a tux, and the slightly rumpled hair coupled with the battle scars made him look rugged and a little dangerous. Yet somehow he fit right in.

One of the tallest and biggest men there, Roman had turned heads the minute they walked through the door. She felt an odd sense of pride to be there with a man whom she considered to be by far the sexiest, most gorgeous in the room. Only they weren't there together, she reminded herself. Not in a romantic way. She had no claim to him, nor did she want one. Though she couldn't deny that a tiny part of her, deep down inside, wished she did.

Okay, maybe it wasn't so tiny. And she hated herself for it. For being so weak. And irrational. For wanting a man who did her and her family so wrong. But her body kept betraying her.

Roman glanced her way, saw her watching him, and a sly grin curled his lips. He said something to the man he'd been speaking with then headed her way, and her heart shifted wildly in her chest.

When he took her hand in the limo she'd just

about melted into a puddle on the leather seat. She'd wanted to pull away, and scold him for being so personal, but she just couldn't make herself do it. It was hard enough to fight the desire to launch herself into his arms and hold him.

But he wasn't hers to hold.

Though as he came up next to her, sliding her hand back into his would have felt as natural as breathing.

Damn him.

"See something you like?" he asked, a suggestive lilt in his tone. One that she was sure was meant to rattle her cage. And it worked.

She gestured randomly in the direction he'd come from, sighed wistfully and said, "Yes, but I think he's married."

Roman threw his head back and laughed. "You're a terrible liar."

Yes, she was, and he knew her too well. She had to fight the irrational urge to lean in close, so that their arms touched.

Back in the old days Roman had never been shy about physical affection in public. He'd always held her hand, no matter where they were.

When she started college she hadn't had a whole lot of sexual experience. Too many times she'd been deceived by men who were only interested in her money and family name. Trust had been a difficult concept to grasp back then. And though she had sacrificed her innocence to one of the men before Roman, she had never surrendered her heart. Sex had been something fun to do, but not emotionally satisfying. She had never come close to connecting emotionally to anyone the way she had with Roman. When they'd finally crossed the line from friends to lovers, she'd been so ready, and so desperately in love with him, making love had been truly magical.

And she had the sneaking suspicion that it still would be, not that she would ever find out.

"Are you having a good time?" she asked him.

"Better than I thought I would. I'm not big on large crowds."

"Then why did you come?"

"I couldn't let the most beautiful woman here show up without a date."

She glared at him, though a smile hovered just below the surface. "This is *not* a date."

He shrugged. "So you keep saying."

She heard someone call her name and looked away from Roman to see Dax Caufield, the newest addition to the state senate, making a beeline for them, flashing that renowned campaign smile. Dax was a typical politician, but a decent guy. She had no doubt that with his good looks and charm he would eventually work his way up the Washington food chain. Though she didn't agree with all of his politics, in a world where lies and half-truths were almost expected, he seemed to be a genuinely good and honest man who believed in his positions. He could be a little overbearing, and a touch arrogant, but that usually went along with the territory. He always struck her as honest and morally sound, so much so that for a short time, for his current state senate seat, she had been an assistant campaign manager. Working behind the scenes, using her experience as an event planner, she'd arranged most of his local speaking engagements and fund-raising events, though it had been the volunteers who did the majority of the work. If there was one thing she excelled at, it was delegation. And because Dax was so popular and well liked, finding people to help had never been an issue.

Still, though he was very attractive and charismatic, he couldn't hold a candle to Roman.

"Grace!" he said, beaming as he gave her a hug and a kiss on the cheek. "I'm so glad you could be here!"

"I wouldn't have missed it," she said, and turned to Roman. "Roman, this is State Senator Dax Caufield. He sponsored this event."

"Roman Slater," Dax said, vigorously shaking Roman's hand. "It's an honor to meet you. I've heard good things about you. And let me say thank you for your service."

Roman nodded, but didn't smile. He was typically rather gregarious but something in his eyes said Dax had rubbed him the wrong way. She was curious to know why, since Roman didn't even know him.

Dax hooked an arm around Gracie's shoulders and told Roman, "This woman is a godsend. She was indispensable during my campaign and she helped to plan this event. I don't know what I would have done without her."

"I think you may be exaggerating a little," Grace said with a smile. "But I did what I could to help."

"It's a privilege to have a true war hero with us tonight," Dax told Roman.

"Every soldier is a hero," Roman said sharply. "And deserves the same honor."

His tone took Gracie aback, but before the situation could get awkward, or escalate, someone called to Dax and he turned his attention to Gracie, his smile never wavering. "I'd like to speak with you later about a few ideas I had for the foundation. In the meantime work your magic."

Gracie smiled. "You know I will."

He winked, then said to Roman, "Have a good time."

When he was gone, Roman said, "I don't like that guy."

Puzzled, Gracie asked, "Why?"

Frowning, he shrugged. "Just a feeling. And what did he mean by work your magic?"

"Let's just say that I have a gift for fund-raising."

Roman looked around. "Then you've got your

work cut out for you. This is quite the guest list. Is there anyone here who isn't rich and famous?"

"Not at ten grand a ticket."

His brows tipped upward. "Is that what I'm paying to be here?"

"Not exactly. I pulled some strings."

For the next half hour or so Gracie introduced Roman around and word spread fast of the "genuine" war hero in their midst. At one point she completely lost track of him, only to see him later on the dance floor with a very popular and very young Hollywood starlet. They were talking and laughing, and she was looking as if she wanted to eat Roman up as a midnight snack.

A wave of jealousy gripped Gracie so intensely she felt like throwing up.

What was wrong with her? She had no right to be jealous. She had no right to feel anything at all. She knew for a fact that Roman was single, so it only made sense that he would socialize and flirt. And it wasn't as if he was there as her real date. She'd said it herself: they were only there as acquaintances.

But knowing that didn't make her feel any better. In fact, it only made her feel worse.

Roman glanced over and caught her watching before she could avert her eyes. So when she did look away, it appeared as if she was trying not to get caught staring. Which of course was exactly the case.

She just couldn't seem to win tonight.

"Hey, you!"

She turned to find her sister Eve approaching with a dazzling smile filled with so much love and affection it warmed Gracie's heart. While Gracie favored their mother's side of the family, Eve was a Winchester through and through. Tall, athletic and elegantly beautiful, Eve had the trademark Winchester green eyes and a dazzling smile. Her hair was perfect, her makeup flawless, and her dress sleek and stylish. No one who didn't know her would guess that underneath the glamorous facade lurked a ruthless businesswoman. Nor would they know that despite her svelte figure, she would soon be trading her sleek size-zero wardrobe for maternity clothes, which had inspired Gracie to consider a designer maternity line of her own. "Hey back, beautiful! You're positively glowing."

Eve hugged her and air-kissed her on each cheek. "And you look lovely as always. Is that dress one of your designs?"

Grace shook her head. "It's Armani."

As much as she loved her own fashions, to wear them to a function for charity felt arrogant and tacky, as though she was a walking billboard for herself. She was proud of her accomplishments, but too humble to be so forward and flashy.

"How have you been feeling?" she asked Eve.

"Pretty good. A little queasy in the mornings, and I've been tired, but I can't complain."

Gracie gazed around the room looking for her soon-to-be brother-in-law. Though he and Eve had been through a rough time, it had only brought them closer together, and made their love for each other and their commitment to their relationship that much stronger. In a way she envied her sisters for finding the loves of their lives. Had it not been for Roman's deceit, she might be married with a family of her own. She'd dated casually over the years, but always made building her business her main priority. She'd always just assumed that when the right one came along, she would know. She would feel that spark of excitement and attraction. The one she'd felt the first time she laid eyes on Roman all those years ago.

But she hadn't even come close.

"Is Brooks here?" she asked her sister.

"He was called out of town on business. But he'll be back for the party at the children's hospital site Sunday. Everyone's excited to see the progress being made on the construction."

"I really hoped that Nora and Reid would be here, so I could thank him." Reid Chamberlain, her future brother-in-law, owned the hotel and had graciously donated the ballroom for the night, as well as posh rooms to the foundation's most generous out-of-town guests.

Eve put a hand on Gracie's shoulder and then asked in a hushed voice, "How are you holding up, baby? Are you all right?"

Holding up? The question struck her as odd, since Eve knew that Gracie loved formal functions. Especially fund-raisers. Schmoozing with the wealthy and divesting them of their inheritances and trust fund money were skills she excelled at. "Fine, why?"

"It must be difficult seeing Roman here. I didn't even know he was on the guest list."

Oh, *that*. She winced a little. How was she supposed to explain this one?

"I suppose it's fitting considering his military status. And his financial success. He's certainly made a name for himself in the past two years. It's hard not to be impressed."

It was very impressive, but for Gracie not at all surprising. She'd always known that someday he would be an incredible success. He had been as driven and dedicated to his studies and his career as Gracie. It was one of the reasons they had connected so instantly in college.

"He actually wasn't on the guest list," she said.

Eve's brow wrinkled with confusion. "Oh. He came as someone's guest?"

"Um, yeah." Gracie hoped she would leave it at that. But of course she didn't. "Whose?"

"Well…"

Eve folded her arms, narrowed her eyes and flashed that don't-screw-with-me look Gracie had seen countless times growing up, and said in a motherly voice, "Gracie…?"

She had no choice but to fess up. "Me. He came here with me."

Her outrage made Gracie wince. *"Why?"*

"It's not what you think. It's not a date. We aren't back together, or getting back together. It's just business."

"Considering the way he's looking at you right now, I find that a little hard to believe."

Gracie looked over to where Roman was now speaking with one of Hollywood's most well-known power couples and an Illinois state representative. But his eyes were on her. He smiled and winked.

Oh hell. Why did he have to go and do that? Especially in front of her sister.

"I rest my case," Eve said.

Gracie turned back to her sister. "The truth is, Daddy asked me to bring him."

Eve closed her eyes and sighed deeply. "Oh, honey, what is he making you do now?"

Apparently even her sister thought their father's overreaching was inappropriate. "He thinks Roman is up to something and he asked me to…well…"

Eve regarded her pensively. "To what?"

"He was hoping I might be able to find out what Roman is up to. Since he and I were so close before."

Eve was not happy. "Who the hell does he think you are? James Bond?"

"That's exactly what I thought, but he guilted

me into it." As usual. "He said he can't take another scandal."

Eve took her hands. "Honey, I know Daddy is very sick, and his time is limited, but you don't have to do this. Not if it's upsetting to you. There are other ways he can get what he needs. After everything Roman put you through…"

"It's really okay," Gracie said, and realized that she meant it. "He and I have unresolved issues. Maybe it's time we clear the air. And let go of the past."

"So do *you* think Roman is up to something?"

That question had been hounding her all night. "I don't know. He takes full responsibility for the problems he caused us seven years ago, but says that he had nothing to do with spreading the rumors about Daddy's alleged illegitimate children in the media this time around. That Brooks acted on his own with information that Roman warned him hadn't been verified. Has Graham mentioned anything?"

Eve frowned. "We don't talk about Brooks. And they don't talk to each other right now. Graham is still furious with him. But if you want my personal opinion…"

Boy, did she ever. "Please."

"Be careful."

Her sister was right, but as Gracie glanced Roman's way and their eyes met, and she felt that tingly anticipation, she wondered if she was already in way over her head.

Five

After making a full sweep of the ballroom and securing commitments for very generous sums from donors, Gracie found an empty seat with a view of the dance floor and settled back to have a drink. Her third of the night, which was her absolute limit. She was scanning the room to see where Roman might be when she felt a tap on her shoulder. "Would you care to dance?"

Gracie looked up to find Roman standing beside her, and like a dummy said, "Dance?"

"It's what those people over there are doing," he said, gesturing to the dance floor with that wry grin. "I hold you, we sway."

"I know what it is," she said, trying not to smile.

He was only making it worse, poking fun at her like that. And she liked it far too much for her own good. The drink was making her feel fuzzy and loosening her inhibitions. Which couldn't have been worse.

She set it down on the table beside her.

"I'm just not sure I want to."

"If I recall, you loved to dance."

"Are you sure you have room on your ticket?" she asked, since as far as she could tell he had danced with practically every young, single woman here tonight.

"What's the matter, Gracie? Are you jealous?" he asked with a playful look that melted her.

She rolled her eyes. "As if."

He leaned in close, the whisper of his breath caressing her ear. "You know you're the only one I really want to dance with."

Why did he have to say things like that? To have him hold her hand had been tantalizing enough, but the idea of being that close to him, and the feelings it would stir up, terrified her. But he was so handsome and charming that when he offered his arm she took it and let him lead her to the dance floor, knowing that the second he pulled her into his arms she would both regret and love it at the same time.

She really shouldn't have had that third drink.

Feeling his huge hand on her lower back, she braced herself as he eased her in close. Much closer than those other women he'd danced with. And as her breasts brushed against his wide chest she felt her nipples tingle and harden. His grip on her hand was gentle yet firm, and as her other hand came to rest on his biceps, she could feel the hard muscle underneath his tuxedo jacket.

Roman had always been a big guy, but now? There was just so much of him. And it felt good.

Way *too* good. Too much like the old days when keeping their hands off each other had been impossible. Her thigh brushed his and against her will she could feel herself relaxing in his arms. Roman had always been a good dancer, and his injuries didn't seem to have changed that.

As if reading her mind, Roman said, "I seem to recall us doing this a time or two before." He paused, his eyes snagging hers, and then added, "Although not with quite so many clothes on. And not vertically."

Her knees went weak and her cheeks burned. He had to go and remind her, didn't he? Making love with Roman had never been anything but wonderful. They connected in a way that she never had with anyone else. Not before and not since. They would spend hours in bed lying naked together alternating between kissing and making love and just talking. Touching him, running her hands over his body, had always been a favorite pastime that never grew old.

Apparently not even now.

"You're pushing it," she warned him, feeling

dizzy from the musky scent of his aftershave as the rest of the world faded into the background, until it felt as if it was just the two of them there in the ballroom.

"It's the truth," he said. "I know you haven't forgotten."

She wished she could, but what they'd had together had been pretty unforgettable. "Stop trying to seduce me."

A grin tilted the corners of his beautiful mouth. "Is that what I'm doing?"

She cursed the wobble in her voice as she said, "I told you that this isn't a date."

The deep baritone of his voice strummed across her senses and his breath tickled her cheek. "So, no good-night kiss at your doorstep?"

"I picked you up," she reminded him.

"No kiss at mine?"

Since the limo had fetched him at his office, she had no idea where he even lived. Not that it made a difference either way. "No kissing *anywhere*."

"Not even a little one on the cheek?"

It would never stop at just her cheek. And one taste of his lips would destroy her self-control. She was on shaky ground as it was.

His eyes grew dark with desire. "But we were *so* good at it."

She couldn't argue there, and denying it would be a waste of time.

"This is business," she told him, scrambling for a safe topic to explore, one he couldn't turn into a sexual innuendo. "Have you talked to Graham and Brooks about meeting with my father?"

"Did Sutton tell you to ask me that?"

Well, no, not specifically, so it wasn't a lie when she said, "I was just curious."

"But he did ask you to bring me tonight. He wants to keep tabs on me."

To say no would be a lie, and she was a terrible liar. He would see right through her.

"Why would you think that?" she asked instead, answering his question with a question of her own.

He laughed. "So that's a yes."

She blinked. "I didn't say—"

"You didn't have to. I can still read you like a book, Gracie."

Damn him. What was she supposed to say now?

The hand resting on her lower back slipped an inch or so lower and her heart skipped a beat. "Look me in the eye and tell me Sutton didn't put you up to this."

She couldn't do it. She couldn't look him in the eye and lie, and if she looked away he would have his answer. She didn't know what to do.

Curse her damned guilty conscience.

The arm around her tightened and Roman's look went from playful to serious in a heartbeat. "I don't care, Gracie. It doesn't matter why we're here together. Just that we are."

He'd obviously known all along that she'd had ulterior motives, and the fact that he wasn't angry, or at least a little upset with her, meant…what? That he wanted her? Well, that was pretty obvious. The question was, what did she want?

The song ended and she pulled away, out of his arms. And thankfully he let her go. If he had resisted, even a tiny bit, or asked her to dance again, she would have been toast.

"I have people I need to speak with," she said. "But thank you for the dance."

He didn't say a word. He just smiled.

And she ran.

Well, her four-inch heels prevented her from *actually* running, but she did bolt. Right for the bar. Screw her three-drink limit. She needed a strong one right now. She was lusting after a man who only three days ago she'd hated with a passion almost as hot as her desire for him.

One more drink turned into two as she mingled and talked up the wealthiest of the guests in attendance. She ignored Roman, but she could feel his eyes on her. He had her in such a state she found herself at the bar asking for drink number six. And at some point she went back for drink number seven. Which was a very bad idea. By eleven o'clock she was feeling more than a little tipsy. She was fatally attracted to him, and her defenses couldn't be much lower. What the hell had she been thinking?

In an attempt to dull her senses, she'd only amplified her desire and left herself more vulnerable than ever.

Stupid, stupid, stupid.

Dizzy and a little disoriented, she made her way to the ladies' room to freshen up. She sat in the lounge for several minutes to collect herself and guzzled a bottle of water, hoping it might dilute the effects of the alcohol, but when she stood back up she felt more unsteady than ever.

What was she supposed to do now, stumble around the ballroom like a drunken fool?

What the hell had she gotten herself into?

Hating herself for being so careless, she left the ladies' room as gracefully as she could. Roman was waiting for her a few feet from the door, holding his coat and her wrap.

"I had a feeling you would be ready to leave," he said and she could have cried she was so relieved.

"Yes, please."

She braced herself against the wall as he slipped her wrap around her shoulders and put on his coat. He slipped his arm through hers, presumably so that she wouldn't fall over, and led her to the elevator.

"You know what happens when you have more than three drinks. Were you trying to get hammered?"

Yup, he had been watching her. That he knew

her so well should have bothered her, but it didn't. Other than her wounded pride, there wasn't much of anything bothering her right now.

"I'm not hammered," she said, but her mouth couldn't seem to make the words come out just right.

"Liar."

Yep, she was lying.

They took the elevator down to the parking level and she leaned against him, his hard body keeping her upright, but as the doors slid open, and she took a step, she stumbled.

"You're going to break a leg in those heels," he said.

"Am not," she argued, stumbling again, clutching his arm for balance. In a flash of movement that left her dizzy and disoriented, he scooped her up into his arms. She let out a startled squeak and wrapped her arms around his neck. "I can walk."

"Barely," he said, sounding amused. He carried her to the limo and helped her inside. Then he disappeared. She looked around, confused. Was he sending her home alone?

He was back several seconds later carrying her clutch and one of her shoes. She looked down and saw that her left foot was bare.

Huh. She hadn't even felt the shoe fall off.

He climbed in and sat across from her. "Lose something?"

"Thanks," she said, as he dropped her things on the seat beside her.

The limo started to move and she closed her eyes.

Bad idea. The interior of the vehicle began to spin around her. She clutched the edge of the seat and opened them again, but it didn't help much.

Roman regarded her sternly. "You're not going to be sick, are you?"

She shook her head, which made the spinning worse. "I may be a *little* drunk."

"You think?"

The seat shifted underneath her, but then she realized it was her body shifting and righted herself. "No, that's a lie," she said, her words slurred. "I'm definitely hammered."

"Are you sure you're not going to be sick?"

"I'm not sure of anything right now." This time, when she closed her eyes, she didn't open them again.

After a night of strange, vivid dreams about Roman, Gracie woke slowly the next morning, a drum pounding in her temples, wondering how the heck, and when the heck, she had gotten home. Her throat was dry and her tongue felt thick and as she pried her eyes open and took in her completely unfamiliar surroundings, she realized she *wasn't* at home. She was...

Where the hell was she?

She blinked the sleep from her eyes and sat up in bed, the movement sending a shaft of pain through her head. Nothing looked familiar.

She spotted a sheath of apricot silk draped over a chair across the room. It was the dress she'd worn the night before. And then she realized that all she had on were her strapless push-up bra and matching panties.

Oh God, what had she done? And where the *hell* was she?

She closed her eyes against the raging pain in her skull and groaned, trying to piece together what had happened last night. The last thing she remembered was Roman carrying her to the limo. Everything after that was pretty much a blur.

Had he taken her home with him?

At the foot of the bed lay a pair of pajama bottoms and T-shirt big enough to fit two of her, and on the bedside table sat a glass of water and two pain-reliever tablets. At least, she was guessing that's what they were. They could have been poison for all she knew, but death right now would be a welcome reprieve from the pain.

She gobbled them down and chugged the entire glass as she glanced around the room. It was decorated in earth tones with splashes of color here and there. The room was neither masculine nor feminine, which told her it was probably a spare. Through an open door she could see the bathroom, and guessed that the closed door next to it was a closet.

She pushed herself to get out of bed and change when what she really wanted to do was lie back down and sleep off the pounding in her head. The T-shirt hung down to her knees and thankfully the pajama bottoms had a drawstring because otherwise they would have been around her ankles. She looked out the window to a very cushy subdivision of midsize homes on decent-size lots. She had no clue where it was geographically. It looked cold and dreary out.

She didn't doubt that Roman could afford a much bigger home, in a much swankier neighborhood, but he had never been into appearances. He had always been a practical man, and she could see that hadn't changed.

In the bathroom she found a toothbrush still in the package and an unopened tube of toothpaste. And when she looked in the mirror she cringed. Her hair was a disaster, sticking every which way, and her mascara was smudged around her eyes. She looked like a deranged raccoon.

She found a hairbrush in one of the drawers and did what she could to her tattered blond locks and used the washcloth hanging on the towel rack to fix her face.

Honestly it wasn't much help. Her excessive behavior was clear in her baggy eyes and pale complexion.

Oh well. Roman had seen her in worse shape than this before.

She brushed her teeth and refilled the water

glass two more times, drinking more slowly. She didn't feel sick, but she didn't feel great, either. If she hadn't already barfed—and oh did she hope she hadn't—it was still a possibility.

With no hope of looking even halfway decent, she opened the bedroom door. The scent of coffee led her down the stairs to an open-concept living and dining room and a functional kitchen.

She found Roman lounging on a leather sectional wearing a long-sleeved camouflage thermal shirt and black running pants, his bare feet propped on a familiar-looking coffee table. He was reading the newspaper and a football game played on the flat-screen television across the room.

"Do I smell coffee?" she said.

He glanced up at her and smiled. "You do. The last time I checked on you, you were stirring so I made a fresh pot."

He'd checked on her. How sweet was that? Not that she needed to be checked on. She was used to living alone. But still…

"Would you like a cup?"

"Please. A really big one." She needed the caffeine to shake the blazing headache.

He eyed her questioningly. "Think your stomach can take it?"

"If I don't have a cup, my head might explode. Unless you have something more direct, like an IV."

He laughed, the deep baritone strumming across

every nerve in her body. Even in her compromised state it made her already-wobbly knees knock a little harder. "Have a seat," he said, pushing up off the couch. "One black coffee coming right up."

She took a seat on the other end of the couch from where he'd been sitting, her body sinking into the plush leather, and watched him as he pulled a mug down from the cupboard over the coffeemaker and poured.

"Did you see the pills I left you?" he asked.

"Yes, thank you. And the things in the bathroom."

He carried the cup to her. "Hungry?"

At the thought of food, her stomach turned and she shook her head.

Bad move.

Her temples screamed and she told him, "One thing at a time."

The superstrong brew burned her tongue, but it tasted amazing. Definitely what she needed. This wasn't the first time he'd nursed her through a hangover. Not even close. And he still knew just what to do. How to make her feel better. And he still cared after all this time.

"So, what happened last night? Aside from me getting drunk?"

He sat back down, taking up so much space it was ridiculous. When had he gotten so...wide? His biceps bulged against the sleeves of his shirt and his thighs were ridiculously muscular. "What do you remember?"

"After we left the hotel? I vaguely recall the limo ride, and after that, nothing. Why did you bring me here instead of taking me home?" Or maybe she didn't want to know.

"I did take you home, but without the passcode I couldn't get you into your apartment. The doorman wasn't much help."

She winced a little at the idea of Dale, the night doorman, seeing her that way.

"How did I end up out of my dress?" she asked.

"You don't remember?"

Cautiously she said, "No."

"Damn," he said, shaking his head, a frown cutting deep into his brow. "Sex that wild, I was sure you would remember."

She gasped, her eyes went wide and her heart stalled in her chest. "We did not!"

"Relax. I'm kidding," he said with a chuckle. "Nothing happened."

Was that disappointment she just felt? Nah, it couldn't be. Besides, if she was going to sleep with him she would like to actually remember it.

If? Oh my God, there was no *if*. She wasn't going to sleep with him. Ever.

Yeah, Gracie, you just keep telling yourself that.

"So why did I wake up in my underwear?"

"I helped you out of your dress and into bed. In the dark, so I didn't see anything."

She narrowed her eyes at him. "Really?"

He grinned. "That's my story and I'm sticking to it."

He was so lying.

"Not that I haven't seen it all before," he added.

True, and her body hadn't changed much in the past seven years. But his sure had, and what she wouldn't give to see him out of his clothes.

"You did try to jump me on the limo ride home, though," he said, and then added with a grin, "Still limber as ever."

Six

"I did not!" Gracie said, looking scandalized. And she was sexy as hell wearing his clothes. She was sexy wearing anything, but seeing her in the oversize shirt stirred up distinct memories. Though he preferred to see her wearing nothing at all.

"Oh yes you did," he told her. She had climbed into his lap and tried to kiss him, and as much as Roman had wanted to kiss her back, he would never take advantage of any woman in such a compromised state. If she was going to kiss him—and he didn't doubt that she would—she was going to be sober. And *she* would come to *him*. "I practically had to beat you off with a stick."

She glared at him.

He laughed. "Okay, I'm lying about the stick part, but you did put the moves on me. You were all hot and bothered."

"I'm sorry," she said with a wince.

Sorry? Last night had been the most fun he'd had in ages. The best part had been watching Gracie watch him dancing with all of those young, beautiful women, knowing she was crawling out of her skin with jealousy.

And the worst part had been watching that Dax character ogling her. That guy had his sights on Gracie, and not just for her philanthropic abilities. Roman had watched him watching her, and could tell the state senator had known as well as Roman that she'd been overdoing it on the drinks. So when Gracie left the ballroom, and Dax followed her, Roman had followed him. He'd never cared much for politicians, and that man had bad news written all over him, so Roman wasn't surprised to find him hovering around the general vicinity of the ladies' lounge.

Rather than allowing Gracie to find herself in a compromising position—and he'd had no doubt about the senator's intentions—he'd collected their coats and headed for the lounge hoping Gracie hadn't already been caught up in the man's web. Dax was still standing there looking irritated and impatient, glancing at his watch. When he saw Roman approach he'd flashed a phony smile.

"Roman!" he'd said, as though they were old friends.

As if.

"Seems like a man in your position wouldn't want to be caught hanging out around the ladies' room," Roman had told him.

Dax had laughed, but there was an uncomfortable edge to his voice when he said, "Just taking a breather."

They both knew that was bullshit. And Roman had never been one to sugarcoat the truth. "This breather wouldn't have anything to do with the fact that Gracie is in there, would it? Or that she's drunk?"

The man's smile had wavered and he'd puffed out his chest. He'd known he'd been busted. But Dax stood several inches shorter than Roman, and was in what could only be considered average physical shape. Roman could take him out with one solid crack to the jaw. Not that he would hit anyone unprovoked, but damn would it have felt good to knock that smug smile off his face.

"Are you her keeper?" Dax had asked him.

"Try me and find out," Roman had said, and his words had taken Dax back a step. As Roman had assumed, he was all talk.

He'd held both hands up in defense. "I just wanted to be sure she made it home safely. But clearly she's in good hands."

Yeah, the only hands she would have anything to do with that night. And when she'd stumbled out of the lounge a few minutes later Roman had gotten her the hell out of there.

"I never get that drunk," Gracie said now. "Not off four drinks."

Is that what she thought she'd had? Damn, she must have been worse off than she realized. "Hate to tell you, sweetheart, but you had more than four."

She frowned. "I did?"

"I saw you hit the bar at least six times."

Her eyes went wide again "*Six?* I did not!"

"Oh yes you did. You were knocking them back like a woman on a mission."

"Why didn't you stop me?"

"Because you're stubborn as hell and you wouldn't have listened. Knowing you, it probably would have made you drink more."

Her pained look said he was right.

"What did you eat yesterday?" he asked her. He couldn't even count how many times in the past he'd had to remind her to eat, and sometimes go so far as force-feeding her. She'd always been so busy and he doubted that had changed much.

She gave it some thought. "Breakfast. *Maybe?*"

"Maybe?"

"It was a busy day."

"You didn't eat at the fund-raiser?"

She shook her head. "Please tell me I didn't make a fool of myself."

"No, but that Dax character had his sights set on you. I don't like him."

"I worked on his campaign. He's a decent guy."

"A decent guy who wants to get in your pants. Or panties. And by the way, you look good in pink lace."

She narrowed her eyes at him. "I thought you said it was dark."

"It was, but I see really well in the dark." She had been so out of it, he'd had to carry her into the house and up the stairs. And with the light streaming in from the hallway, it hadn't left a whole lot to the imagination.

"Would it be too much to ask for a ride home?" she asked. "Or I can take a cab. Honestly I don't even know where I am."

"You're not going anywhere until you get some food in your stomach," he said.

"I'm not quite there yet. My head is still pounding and my stomach feels iffy."

"Then sit back and relax. How about a cold compress for your head?"

"Are you sure you don't mind? If you have things to do…"

"It's Saturday. There's nothing that can't wait."

"I usually work Saturday," she said. "And Sunday. Mostly on charity stuff."

Clearly they shared the same work ethic. "Not today. Today you're going to relax."

"I guess I could stay for a little while," she said. "And the compress couldn't hurt."

"Lie down and make yourself comfortable. I'll get it."

He pushed himself up off the sofa and the effort made his left leg, which was more titanium than bone, ache. He had been in bad shape when he and his men had been rescued. His femur, which had been shattered in one of many beatings, had become infected. Had it been a day or two longer he probably would have lost his entire leg from the hip down. A week and he would have gone septic. The rescue had come just in the nick of time.

After several surgeries and months of rehabilitation he still walked with a limp, and was in near constant pain, but he was alive.

He grabbed a compress from the freezer and carried it back to her. She was stretched out, her hands folded across her chest, eyes closed, snoring softly.

He very gently set the compress across her forehead and she didn't rouse. If she was anything like him she didn't get more than five or six hours of sleep a night, so every moment of rest counted and he didn't wake her. Or climb on the couch beside her—which would have carried the very real risk of getting slapped. Instead he went upstairs to take a shower. And considering the ache in his groin, it would probably be a cold one.

Despite his attraction to her, she was a Winchester, and the running feud between himself and her family would always be there. Gracie was very close to her sisters and parents, who all despised him. He'd seen the expression on Eve's face last night when she looked over at him. Indignation. Raw and fresh. They would never accept him, and he would never do anything to alter their family dynamic.

But if it was just sex…

The only problem was that with Gracie, it had never been *just sex*.

Roman shaved, showered and pulled on a pair of boxer briefs. Having lived alone for so long, it hadn't occurred to him that he should have shut the bedroom door. Not until he heard a breathy "Oh my God" and looked up to see Gracie standing in the doorway.

"You have tattoos," Gracie said, her eyes so fixed on the ink branding his arms that she barely noticed he was in his underwear.

Okay, yeah, that was a lie. She'd noticed. And though he'd always been in great shape physically, now? He was ridiculously buff.

On his enormous left biceps, spanning from the edge of his shoulder to the crook of his arm, he had a very scary-looking skull and crossbones. The skull wore an army helmet, and the bones were actually military rifles. The right biceps bore a flowing American flag with red barbed wire for stripes.

She wanted to touch them. His biceps and his wide shoulders. And every other inch of his body.

"You like tattoos?" he asked, though the words barely made it through the fog that had settled in her brain. And he didn't look the least bit scandalized that she was seeing him this way. He'd never been shy about his body.

He had nothing to be shy about.

Transfixed, she nodded. But the real treat was when he said, "There's more," and turned.

An American eagle in flight spanned the entire width of his back, the tips of the bird's wings flirting with the edges of his tattooed arms. In its razor-sharp talons it clutched a banner that said Death Before Dishonor.

She couldn't stop a very breathy-sounding "wow" from escaping her lips.

Wearing a slightly crooked smile, he looked back over his shoulder at her. "See something you like?"

Did she ever. The bird was so lifelike she imagined she would actually feel the silky softness of the feathers if she touched Roman's back. Then he was getting closer, but he wasn't the one moving. Her feet were carrying her across the room to where he stood, then her hands were reaching out.

She felt possessed. And she was—by lust. By a need so intense her breasts ached and her heart pounded. She flattened both hands against his skin at the level of the eagle's breast and she could swear she felt Roman shiver. She slid her hands upward, across the wings to his shoulders.

"Gracie," he said, in a voice gravelly and low. "If you keep that up…"

He didn't have to finish his sentence; she knew exactly what he was going to say, and she was already too far gone. Now that she had touched him she couldn't stop. The ache pulsed downward and settled between her thighs and she could feel herself getting wet. His skin was hot and smooth against her palms as she slid them upward across the eagle's wings.

Over his shoulders.

Down his arms.

He moaned softly and uttered her name, and all she could think was *mine*. She wanted him, and nothing was going to stop her from having him this time.

She wrapped her arms around him and pressed her cheek to his wide back, threading her fingers through the thick, crisp hair on his chest, his hard nipples tickling her palms.

His head fell back and he cursed under his breath as she hugged herself close to his body, but it wasn't close enough. She wanted to crawl inside of him, be a part of his being. A part of his soul.

He had always been a part of hers. Maybe that was why his betrayal had hurt so much.

"Last warning," he told her. He was still holding back, but he was wasting his time. She dragged her nails down his chest to his stomach, gently, so it was barely more than a tease, then slipped her hands under the waistband of his shorts. He groaned as she wrapped one hand around his erection. He was solid and hot in her hand. She stroked him, gently at first, then she squeezed.

With a throaty growl he spun her around to face her, then wrapped his arms around her and lifted her right off her feet. She wrapped her arms around his neck and her legs around his hips, and when their lips met and their tongues tangled in a desperate kiss, it felt just like it had that first time so many years ago.

They fell onto the bed, Roman on top of her. He grabbed the hem of her T-shirt and pulled it up over her head. She moaned as he buried his face in her cleavage and tugged the cups of her bra down.

"You're so beautiful," he said, teasing the tip of one breast with his tongue, then nipping just hard enough to make her gasp. After all this time he still knew what to do to drive her crazy. He did the same to the other side, then he unfastened her bra with an adept flick of his fingers, pulled it off her and tossed it somewhere over his shoulder. Then he kissed her again, the hair on his chest tickling her nipples in the most tantalizing way.

She yanked his shorts off over his hips and used her feet to push them down his legs, desperate to feel him inside her. There was a fire building at her core, an ember burning hot on the verge of igniting.

He rose up on his knees, stripping her out of her pants and underwear in one swift motion, and grabbed a condom out of the drawer of the bedside table. Tearing the packet open with his teeth, he wasted no time rolling the condom on. Then he was back on top of her, his weight sinking her into the covers. He teased her first, sliding his erection against her. She was so slick and sensitive she probably could have climaxed just like that. But then he stopped, pulling back slightly. If he stopped now she was afraid that she actually might die from the ache building inside her.

She grabbed his muscular backside, and though she had never been one to beg she said, *"Please, don't stop."*

He grinned down at her, eyes glazed, his lids heavy. "Not a chance in hell."

His eyes locked on hers as he slowly entered her, giving her just an inch or two before pulling back again. Slow and gentle and sweet. But she didn't want slow. She needed him inside her now.

Digging into his buttocks with her nails, she thrust her hips upward against him. She cried out as he sank as deep as he could go. Roman moaned and buried his head in the crook of her neck as he cursed and told her with gritted teeth, "Slow down."

But she couldn't. She didn't want to slow down. She arched up to meet each of his thrusts, slipping easily into the rhythm they had mastered so long ago, their bodies so perfectly in sync it was almost as if they were one person.

Across the room, in the mirror above his chest of drawers, she could see their reflection. She lay beneath him, her legs hooked tightly around his hips, his muscular backside flexing with every thrust. It was the hottest, most arousing thing she had ever seen, and her muscles instantly began to coil and tighten. He must have felt it, too. He groaned and tunneled his fingers through her hair, kissed her hard as she reached a crest of pleasure that left her weak and breathless.

Moaning as her muscles gripped and pulsed around him, Roman was only seconds behind her. He picked up speed and pressed his forehead to hers, eyes squeezing shut as every muscle in his body tensed. "Gracie," he moaned as he climaxed, holding her so close and so tight she could almost feel the pleasure coursing through him.

Shuddering and gasping for air, they lay like that, wrapped in each other's arms, their bodies still intimately joined. And though she tried to fight it, feelings of affection threatened to overwhelm her.

This was just good sex, she told herself. No, not good sex. Fantastic sex. Mind-blowing, earth-shattering, out-of-this-universe sex.

But still just sex.

Then he lifted his head and looked deep in her eyes, teased the tip of her nose with his own and smiled, and her insides went all gooey again. But not gooey enough to say or do something she would later regret.

She was a woman who kept her heart carefully guarded and locked up tight. He used to have the key, but it would do him no good. It had taken so long for her broken heart to repair itself that the lock had rusted shut. And she refused to let anyone, especially him, break it again.

Besides, even if she wanted it to be more, even if she could someday forgive and trust him again, her family never would. Sure, he was charming and funny and great in bed, but he had given her no reason to trust him. And far too many reasons not to.

Seven

Grace stood with her sisters amidst the crowd at the construction site of the new children's hospital, shivering under her cashmere coat. The reception for donors was set to begin in just a few minutes and she had serious mixed feelings about being there. After all, the Newport brothers were naming the hospital after Cynthia Newport. The woman with whom her father had had an affair and an illegitimate child. But Carson was her half-brother, and Eve was engaged to his brother Graham, so how could she not be there for them? The project was being funded almost entirely by the Newports.

She turned to scan the crowd to see many familiar faces. Nash Chamberlain and his wife, Gina.

And of course Georgia and Carson. Even Dr. Lucinda Walsh and Josh Calhoun were in town. Brilliant cancer specialist that Lucinda was, Gracie and her sisters had hoped that she would remain their father's caretaker for the duration of his illness, but her love for Josh had taken her from Chicago to his dairy farm in Iowa, where, Gracie had heard, she was taking over the oncology department at a local hospital. Josh, with his long hair, rugged good looks and cowboy hat, was a quintessential cowboy.

"Of course they had to pick the coldest day of the year for this," Nora said, pulling her collar up against the bitter cold wind that poured in through openings that would soon be windows. "The windchill has to be ten below zero."

Eve pulled out her phone and checked. "Close, fifteen degrees."

"I feel warmer already," she joked.

"Have you talked to Mom?" Nora asked Eve.

Eve frowned and shook her head. Despite their parents' divorce, and their father's very public reputation for womanizing, the news that he had fathered a child with Cynthia Newport had hit their mother, Celeste, pretty hard. It had also been difficult for her to accept that Eve was in love with Graham, and that her grandchild would have the Newport name.

"She'll come around," Nora said, wrapping her arm around Eve's waist and giving her a squeeze.

"I know," Eve said, clearly holding back tears. "It still hurts, though."

Of the three sisters Eve was by far the toughest of the bunch, but Gracie had the feeling her hormones were out of whack from her pregnancy and making her weepy.

"I'm sorry," Nora said. "I shouldn't have brought it up."

"It will all work out," Eve said, but not with her usual confidence. "It will just take time."

There was a moment of silence, then Nora asked Gracie, "So how did the fund-raiser go Friday? I'm sorry I couldn't be there but the wedding plans have me chasing my own tail."

"It was great," she told her sister, but it was the memory of Saturday that was making her feel all warm and toasty under her coat.

Nora frowned. "That's it? Just *great*? No juicy gossip to share?"

"Honestly the whole night is kind of a blur." She glanced over at Eve, who was looking straight ahead with a wry smile on her face. Had she said something to Nora about Gracie being there with Roman? And the fact that she'd gotten drunk.

If she had, or if someone else had mentioned it, Nora didn't let on.

"Did you meet your fund-raising goal?" Nora asked her, and Gracie wished she would just let it go.

"I haven't talked to Dax yet, so I'm not sure."

Nora looked at her funny. "I thought you would be all over it Saturday."

She'd been all over something, but it wasn't fund-raising.

"It's a busy time for me at work," she said, hoping Nora would drop the subject. She didn't want to think about the fund-raiser or work or anything else. She didn't even want to be here today. Where she wanted to be was back in bed with Roman. And at the same time, the reality of how quickly and effortlessly they had reconnected scared the hell out of her. This was not a good idea, this thing they had started. It had never been her intention to sleep with him. Not that it wasn't some of the best sex she'd ever had in her life. But they had crossed a line, and she was afraid that she would never be able to cross back over it to where she was before. She wasn't even sure if she wanted to go back, and that was probably the scariest thing of all.

She wanted to trust him, and believe that he had nothing to do with the recent smear campaign targeting her father, but that didn't erase what had happened seven years ago. He had taken responsibility for his mistake, and his time in the service went a long way to prove his character. She wished she could just let it go, but it still lingered there somewhere in the back of her mind. She wasn't sure if that residual little sliver of doubt would ever completely go away. And that lack of trust would eventually become their undoing.

Or maybe she would get over it and they would live happily ever after. If that was even what he wanted. Or what she wanted. Was she obsessing over something that he might not even want? Was she assuming things that had no basis in reality?

It was all so confusing.

"Well, if it isn't the Winchester girls," someone said from behind them and they turned to see Brooks Newport, smug as usual, walking toward them.

"Oh great," she heard Eve mutter under her breath, but not quietly enough.

Brooks, with acid in his voice, said, "Sorry, I didn't catch that."

Gracie was typically nonconfrontational, and tried to stay out of family spats, but she was feeling particularly snarky today. "Grow up, Brooks."

Her sisters both turned to her, looking as if they couldn't believe that had come out of her mouth. Brooks looked a little taken aback himself, but he recovered quickly.

"So the spoiled little heiress has a voice."

"She does," Gracie said, and though she had never been comfortable using profanity, she calmly, but forcefully, said, "and she's sick of your bullshit intimidations. This is a special day for your family and your inability to behave like an adult does a great disservice to your brothers and disrespects your mother's memory."

He obviously didn't like being called out as the immature, narcissistic ass that he was. "Your father is the one who disrespected my mother," he said smugly, with a top-that look.

So she did. "And that makes you no better than he is."

Brooks blinked, and she could see that the comment stung. Well, good. She hoped it would make him stop and think about his actions.

She could see the wheels in his head spinning, but before the situation could escalate further, Carson appeared at his brother's side.

"We're getting ready to start," he told Brooks.

Brooks looked at Gracie and her sisters, as if he wanted to say something more, but then turned and stalked away.

"Everything okay here?" Carson asked his half sisters.

"Fine," Gracie said. "Brooks was just being Brooks."

Carson shook his head sadly. "I wish I knew why he's so bitter. I understand his anger toward Sutton, but there's no reason to drag the three of you into it. I'm sorry if he upset you."

"I think I speak for me and my sisters when I say we're over it," Gracie told him.

"You're my family," Carson said. "I don't want Brooks's behavior to have a negative impact on that."

"Brooks's behavior has no bearing on our connection to you," Nora told him. "Family is family."

Gracie figured that they had proved that by accepting Carson as their sibling, despite the extramarital affair that was responsible for his existence. Sutton's actions were in no way Carson's fault, and it wasn't fair to blame him for their father's poor judgment.

"I have to go," Carson said. "Maybe we can talk more afterward."

When he was gone, Eve looked at Gracie and asked, "Wow, what's gotten into you today?"

Riding on the edge of a guilty conscience, Gracie asked, "Was it wrong of me to stand up to Brooks?"

Nora laughed. "Heck no. He expected you to defend Sutton, and when you didn't he had no idea what to say."

"You blindsided him," Eve said. "And it was thoroughly amusing."

Gracie's phone buzzed with a text. She pulled it out of her pocket and saw that she had a message from Roman. She was almost afraid to open it on the chance that he would say their encounter had been a mistake, and there was just too much bad blood between them to make even a sexual relationship work. Because she saw no harm in occasionally having a warm body to cozy up to on cold nights. She had needs and Roman was pretty damned good at fulfilling them.

Occasionally.

Her heart pounded as she punched in the code on her phone and the text popped up on the screen.

Dinner at my place? Then a little dessert?

She couldn't suppress the smile curling her lips. She'd been worried for no reason. He obviously was still interested. As excited as she was, and as much as she wanted to see him, she had the distinct feeling that her life was about to get very complicated.

With the guarantee that Sutton was about to reveal information about the identity of their real father, Roman finally talked both Graham and Brooks into a meeting with the dying tycoon. Which was how, the following Friday, Roman found himself back at the Winchester estate. Once again against his will and better judgment. He just hoped that Sutton would actually deliver this time. According to Grace he hadn't been out of bed in days and she was worried that the cancer, or the treatments, or a combination of both, had begun to affect him mentally. She'd been visiting him daily, and he'd been alternating between being himself, sinking into a deep depression and experiencing fits of irrational anger at the drop of a hat. She said it was a little like Jekyll and Hyde.

Roman didn't even know why he had to be there. When he'd asked Sutton, all he'd gotten back was a very cryptic *To keep the peace*. But if tempers flared and Graham took a shot at his brother, it wasn't Roman's responsibility to stop him. As far as he was concerned Brooks could use a little sense knocked into him. And though Brooks was nothing more than a thug in an expensive suit, he was still a client—and a very lucrative one at that—and Roman was under contract to find their birth father. As far as he'd found, it was as though their mother, Cynthia, in the time before she moved to Chicago, hadn't existed.

Gracie had wanted to join them but her father had forbidden it, and of course she'd backed down instantly. It had always fascinated Roman, the control her father had over her. Gracie on her own, in any other element, was one of the toughest, brightest, most capable women Roman had ever met. She'd certainly never taken any crap from Roman. But bring Daddy into the picture and her backbone mysteriously dissolved.

She'd certainly been aggressive Saturday morning. And Saturday afternoon, and most of Saturday night. He drove her home Sunday morning so she could get ready to attend the hospital reception, then she came back Monday evening and he'd made her dinner. He had talked to her every day since then, but they hadn't seen each other since she left Monday night.

Clearly the fire that burned between them seven years ago had never gone out. But he could feel her holding back. And he understood. He couldn't say for sure that he was still in love with her. But he couldn't say that he *wasn't* in love with her, either. Not that it mattered. She'd made it clear that it was just sex to her. That she could never trust him with her heart again. But they could still be friends.

Friends with benefits. He could live with that.

When he arrived at the Winchester estate Brooks and Graham were already there, and he was surprised to find Carson, their youngest brother, and Sutton's recently confirmed son, standing by his bedside. Sutton held the meeting in his personal suite from his bed. Though Roman had thought he couldn't look much worse than the last time he saw the man, he'd been wrong.

Brooks and Graham stood far from each other, at opposite ends of the room.

"It's about damned time," Brooks snapped at Roman as Sutton's nurse showed him into the room, then reclaimed her seat just outside the door. According to Roman's Rolex he was a minute early.

"Forgive my brother," Graham apologized, looking both irritated and resigned. "I've yet to find anything to kill the bug that crawled up his ass."

The comment earned him a glare from Brooks. Hell, maybe they would come to blows.

Roman took a spot at the foot of the bed between the two men. Just in case.

"Now that we're all here, let's get started," Sutton

said, his voice so weak Roman had to strain to hear him. He was sitting propped up by a mountain of pillows, which Roman suspected was the only thing holding him upright. It reminded him of Gracie in the limo on the way home the other night, and he instantly wanted to smile.

Graham moved to his future father-in-law's side. "Roman tells me that you have information about our father."

"I do."

"I'm a little confused as to why I'm here," Carson said. "I know who my father is. I have no relation to the man you're looking for."

"This concerns your mother, too," Sutton told him.

"So out with it," Brooks snapped, completely insensitive to his rival's fragile condition.

"You all know that I'm a man of my word. Once I've made a promise I will not break it," Sutton said.

"Which is why you never promise anyone anything," Roman told him and Sutton shot him a vague, wry smile.

"But I did once, a long time ago. A promise that until recently I intended to take to my grave." He looked from Brooks to his brother. "One I made to your mother."

"Your word means nothing to me, old man," Brooks ground out. "Just tell us what you know."

"First you have to give me your word that what

I am about to tell you will never leave this room."
He looked to Roman. "All four of you."

"This is business," Roman said. "I would never
divulge to anyone information I obtained in a private meeting with my clients."

Sutton looked to Graham. He nodded and said,
"Of course." Then Graham gave his brother a look
that seemed to say, *Do it or else.*

Brooks grudgingly nodded. "You have my word,
as well."

"First I want you to know that your mother was
an amazing woman. I had never met anyone like
her. And I haven't since."

"And when was that?" Brooks asked.

"She was pregnant with the two of you," Sutton
said. "Pregnant and alone working as a waitress in
a café I went to occasionally. She'd only been working there a week, and she spilled a drink in my lap.
She apologized profusely, then broke down in tears,
so afraid that she would lose her job…" He smiled
vaguely and faded off, as if lost in thought. To anyone who didn't know what a coldhearted and brutal
businessman he was, they might think he was just
an average sentimental old man.

"And?" Brooks snapped after several seconds,
which earned him another look from Graham.
Roman couldn't deny feeling a little irritated, too.
It was obvious that Sutton was in poor shape. Still
Brooks couldn't cut him a break, which said a lot

about his integrity. As in he had none. The man lay dying in front of him, confessing a secret he'd once intended to die with, and Brooks couldn't see past his thirst for revenge. His need to conquer.

But Sutton didn't even seem to notice. Or didn't care.

"Let the man speak," Graham said with a warning tone.

Carson laid a hand on his father's shoulder and in a patient voice said, "Go on, Sutton."

Sutton blinked rapidly and snapped back to the present. "I could see the desperation in her eyes, and that she was carrying a child, or as I later discovered, two children. I left her a generous tip, and couldn't stop thinking about her. When I went back a week later she was working again, and I found that I was happy to see her. But she looked so tired and stressed, as if she carried the weight of the world on her shoulders.

"She thanked me for my generosity the week before. She wouldn't admit it then—she was too proud—but she had been about to lose the room she was renting and that tip was enough to pay her rent for another month. That was before her coworker Gerty took her in. I hung around for a while, until her shift ended, and I invited her to have dinner with me.

"She hesitated of course, worried I had ulterior motives, but I think hunger won out over her pride.

And she ate like she hadn't seen real food in months. It gave me so much satisfaction to help her."

"Why do I find that hard to believe?" Brooks said, but Sutton went on as if he hadn't even heard him.

"I inquired about her pregnancy, and she confessed to me that she hadn't told the father of her unborn twins about the pregnancy before moving to Chicago from Texas to start over. The long hours on her feet were difficult, but it was the only job she could find. But she said that now, since her pregnancy had begun to show, her boss was making noise like she would no longer be an asset. She knew it was only a matter of time before she was fired."

"Isn't that illegal?" Carson asked.

Sutton shook his head. "Not back then. But I admired her courage and fortitude, so I offered her a job." His eyes belied the affection he felt, and maybe still felt, for Cynthia Newport.

"As your *mistress*?" Brooks asked.

"As my secretary. She had no experience. She couldn't even type, but I knew that she would learn and she did. And what started out as a friendship became something more. I helped her as much as I could after you and your brother were born. But we had to keep our relationship a secret."

"Which is how Carson came to be," Graham said, looking to his younger brother.

Brooks glared at Sutton. "That's what womanizers do."

Sutton faced him, looking almost apologetic. "It was more than an affair. We were deeply in love. Your mother was my soul mate. I would have done anything for her. I wanted to divorce Celeste and marry her, but back then I was still under my father-in-law's thumb. He threatened to ruin me financially, and keep my daughter and my unborn child from me. Cynthia couldn't bear to watch that happen. We knew that as long as we were together Celeste's family would never let us be happy. So we were forced to go our separate ways.

"When she discovered she was pregnant with Carson she said nothing, would never confirm that he was mine, so I tried to forget her. I distracted myself with work, and women who meant nothing to me, thinking it would ease the need to be with her. But it never did. I always told myself, maybe someday... Then she died and I lost my chance."

"You claim to have loved her, but you didn't even come to her funeral," Brooks said.

"I couldn't," Sutton said. "It would have caused a scene, and I couldn't do that to her."

Carson shot his brother a look and told Sutton, "I understand."

"The day your mother and I parted ways, she made me promise something, something I had to swear I would take to my grave."

"Yet here we are," Brooks said smugly. "And you claim you're a man of your word?"

"Enough!" Carson snapped at his older brother, and Brooks actually backed down.

Sutton looked so sad when he said, "I don't have much time left, Brooks, and I don't want her secret to die with me. Our personal feelings aside, as her sons, you should know who your mother really was, and what she sacrificed for the two of you. It's all I can do to honor the memory of the woman I never stopped loving."

"What do you mean who she really was?" Graham asked, his brow knit.

"Your mom wasn't who you thought she was. Her real name was Amy Jo Turner."

Eight

The brothers all looked taken aback. "She moved here from Cool Springs, a small town in Texas."

"Son of a bitch," Roman muttered, shaking his head. With the truth out it all made sense. He'd always suspected that Cynthia Newport was an alias, but he could never be sure and his investigation had proven inconclusive. "That explains why I couldn't find anything on her before she moved here."

Sutton's nod seemed to take extreme effort. "She had no choice."

"Why would she change her name and lie about where she's from?" Brooks asked, sounding a little less cocky this time. "Was she a criminal? On the run from the law?"

"She was on the run, but not from the law. She was trying to get away from her father, your grandfather."

Graham frowned. "Why?"

"He was an evil man. A violent and sadistic alcoholic. She told me about the beatings and the emotional abuse..." He shook his head, wincing, as if the words were too painful to speak. "He was a monster."

"She had scars," Graham said. "Physical ones. I remember asking her about them and she brushed it off, said something about being clumsy. I think deep down I knew it was a lie. Maybe I didn't want to know the truth."

"She wasn't clumsy. But she did get careless, and found herself pregnant. She knew he would beat her. Two of her classmates turned up pregnant the previous year, and her father told her that if she ever got herself knocked up, he would take care of the 'problem' himself, with a fist to her stomach. Then he would kill the man who'd violated his daughter.

"She knew that he would do it. For everyone's safety she knew she had to leave. But she couldn't just disappear. She knew he would try to find her. And kill her."

"Jesus," Brooks mumbled as the color leeched from his face, the reality of the situation finally sinking in. "What about her mother?"

"She left when Cynthia was five. She couldn't take the beatings and the abuse any longer."

"And she just left our mother with him? Why?"

"She didn't have a choice. He would have never let her take Cynthia away. And she feared that if she tried, he would kill them both."

"So our mother changed her name," Graham said.

"She did more than change her name. As far as everyone in Cool Springs is concerned, Amy Jo Turner went for a swim in Whisper Lake and never came back out. They found her belongings on the ground at the water's edge, and though they never did find a body, she was assumed dead."

Carson shook his head in disbelief. "Our mother faked her own death?"

Sutton nodded, looking sallow and tired. And so sad.

Knowing the man's reputation as a shameless womanizer, the depth of emotion he was showing in regard to Cynthia blew Roman away. He could hardly believe it, but he actually felt sorry for the man.

"She had no other choice," Sutton told them.

"So what about our father?" Graham asked. "Do you know who he is?"

Sutton shook his head. "She never told me his name, but I know that he lived in the same town. And she told me once that you boys look just like him. I don't doubt that with this new information, Roman will be able to track him down."

As long as Roman had known Sutton, that was the closest thing to praise he'd ever gotten from him.

"Does he even know we exist?" Graham asked.

"She never told him about her pregnancy."

At least now Roman knew why Sutton wanted to keep Gracie out of this meeting. Sutton's dalliances were legend in Chicago. But it would have been awkward, explaining in front of his own daughter how he'd not only cheated on her mother, but had been in love with Cynthia.

As if reading his mind, Sutton looked over to Roman and said, "My daughters can never know about this."

So what the hell was he supposed to tell Gracie when she asked Roman about the meeting? Did Sutton expect him to lie to her? Or would she accept that what was said was confidential? That it was official business and as such he couldn't break privilege. He was a man of his word. Once he made a promise, he would not break it. He'd learned that lesson too late to save his relationship with Gracie, but it was a mistake he would never make again.

Either way, he couldn't tell her.

The brothers were eager for answers, and Roman was eager to finally solve the mystery, but when the other men left, he hung back, hoping to have a word with Sutton alone.

"You have something to say to me?" Sutton asked him when he didn't leave.

Roman stood at the foot of the bed, feet spread, arms folded across his chest. It was an intimidation tactic, and one he did automatically, because he knew that despite being so ill, no one could intimidate the great Sutton Winchester.

"That was good what you did for them," Roman said.

"I didn't do it for them," the older man said, looking so weak and pale Roman worried he might drop dead right there. "I did it to honor Cynthia and her legacy. I couldn't let the truth of who she was die with her."

"You really did love her," Roman said, finding that hard to imagine.

"I've loved deeply, and I lost her. But that was my fault. I never should have let her go, but I did and I've had to live with that. I was torn between being with the woman I loved and losing my family, who I loved just as much. Though I haven't always been good at showing it."

"Yeah, about that. Kudos on the reconnaissance mission you sent Grace on."

He folded his hands in his lap. "You disapprove?"

"That's putting it lightly."

"Everything that I do, every decision I make, is for the good of the family name," Sutton said.

He really was a selfish bastard, wasn't he? Though Roman really should be thanking Sutton. His actions had brought Roman and Gracie back together.

Which, come to think of it, was probably the worst thing he could have done if he wanted Roman out of the picture. Sutton had never approved of him before the first scandal, and he sure as hell never would now. But Sutton had seen Gracie's reaction to Roman that day in his office. She was clearly shaken. Hell, there was no reason for her to even be there, other than to rattle Roman's cage. So why would he take the chance that Gracie and Roman might reunite? Wouldn't he want them as far apart as possible?

And what did that mean exactly?

Roman heard a soft snore and realized that Sutton had fallen asleep.

Dude, it doesn't even matter. Sutton was dying, and Gracie had set very clear parameters for their relationship. They would go back to being good friends, like before, with the added bonus of incredible sex.

What man in his right mind would turn down a deal like that?

Roman didn't call Gracie after the meeting. Which she took to mean that he couldn't talk about what had been discussed. She understood confidentiality agreements. Every one of her employees was required to sign one. The fashion industry was rampant with espionage and backstabbing. It was the nature of the business.

Whatever had happened in there, her father didn't want her to know about it, but she couldn't deny that she was dying of curiosity. Yet she felt torn between wanting the truth and wondering if she was better off in the dark. All she did know for sure was that her father had divulged the information necessary for Roman to continue his search for Graham and Brooks's father. Eve had called to let her know. She just didn't know what that information was.

She had decided that if Sutton wanted her to know, he would tell her. Which was why when Roman picked her up later that evening she didn't bring it up. It would only put him in an uncomfortable position, and she wanted this to be a good night. Though they had spoken on the phone every day since last Sunday, neither had had time to see one another. They'd both been too busy to take the time away from work.

But tonight was all about them. He was taking her to one of the hottest new restaurants in downtown Chicago. And one of the priciest. And he must have been in some sort of hurry because he was driving like a maniac, whipping around corners and going over the speed limit.

"You know that the restaurant isn't going anywhere," she told him, clutching the door as he took a turn at high speed.

Roman glanced her way, a wry grin on his face.

"What's the point of having a sports car if you can't have fun with it?"

"There is a fine line between fun and idiocy," she said, knowing that he had always been a thrill seeker, and fearless, which was probably why he had done so well in black ops.

He whipped around a curve in the road while she held on for dear life. "I'd like to get to dinner alive if it's not too much trouble."

With a smile he slowed and downshifted. Why did she get the feeling he was trying to rattle her chain? And why, deep down, did she kind of like it?

"You used to love going fast," Roman said.

"Then I grew up."

"That's too bad. The Gracie I knew liked to take risks."

She couldn't help but feel defensive. "I've taken tons of risks. My business plan was aggressive, and extremely risky. I invested everything I had into my clothing line."

"I'm not talking about financial risk. Money doesn't count. Money isn't *real*. If you lose it you can always earn it back. A real risk is the possibility of losing something priceless."

She didn't mean to say them, but the words just popped out of her mouth. "Like when you lost me."

She expected a snarky reply or a witty comeback; instead he nodded, eyes forward, voice low, and said, "Yes, just like that."

His words dripped with so much regret her heart hurt. What was wrong with her? She had been looking forward to this night all week. Why was she trying to sabotage it?

"I'm sorry," she said.

"Don't be. It's the truth."

"I know, but—"

"Gracie," he said, reaching over to take her hand. "Don't worry about it. Not a day goes by that I don't think about what I did and regret it. I would take it back if I could. But all I can do now is move forward."

"I want to let it go," she said. "I want to be over it. I want to trust you."

"And you will when you're ready." He gave her hand a squeeze then let go to shift. "Just let it go tonight, so we can have a good time."

"Okay," she said, but still felt lousy for bringing it up in the first place. It was against her nature to hurt people, and when she did, she always felt awful. She was sure that right now she felt far worse for saying what she'd said than he had hearing it. Or maybe not.

They pulled up to the restaurant, a seafood and steak house that was receiving rave reviews, and the valet opened her door. Roman handed over his keys and they walked inside.

It would have made her night if he had taken her hand as they walked in, but friends didn't do that sort of thing. She couldn't be seen with him in public, looking so close and intimate. She could just imagine the chatter and gossip that would surely follow. Honestly it would be better if they weren't seen in public together at all. The last thing she wanted was for this to get complicated.

The hostess greeted Roman by name and took their coats, then led them immediately to a table in a dimly lit enclosed patio away from the chatter, with a stunning view of Lake Michigan. The night sky was clear and the surface of the choppy water shimmered in the moonlight.

A candle illuminated the cloth-covered table, and rose petals lay scattered across the surface. Champagne sat chilling in a silver bucket beside it, and a single long-stem rose lay across her napkin.

Simple and elegant, and it stole her breath. This kind of gesture was the last thing she had expected from a "friend."

Just getting the reservation must have been a feat. She knew for a fact that they were booked months in advance, and anyone getting in on a few days' notice had to have some pull. And they were sitting in the absolute prime seats of the establishment.

Roman had pulled out all of the stops and she had nearly ruined the night with her big mouth, by making him feel bad for something he already clearly regretted. Though she hated to admit it, there were times when bits of her father came out in her own personality. She loved him, and respected him as a businessman. But as a person, he'd done nothing but let her down, and served as a terrible example of how a man should be. Which was probably why she'd been so attracted to Roman. He couldn't have been more different than Sutton in practically every way.

Their waiter, a youngish and very attractive guy—probably a college student—appeared immediately. He greeted Roman by name, offered them each a leather-bound menu and poured the champagne. Without even looking at the menu Roman ordered what had always been her favorite appetizer. Though she considered herself a modern and independent woman, knowing that Roman still knew her so well, she didn't mind that he'd ordered without asking what she wanted.

"To new beginnings," he said, toasting the night with a gentle clink of the delicate crystal flutes.

She took a sip then set her glass down. "I'm curious. How did you get a reservation here?"

"You're not the only one who knows people," he said with a grin, opening his menu. "What are you in the mood for?"

A slow smile curled her lips and he didn't even have to ask what she was thinking.

His eyes growing dark with desire, he said, "Sweetheart, that's dessert."

"Grace!"

Hearing her name being called, she turned to

see Dax approaching their table. Roman frowned. Though she was sure he hadn't meant to, Dax had just killed what had been a very special, and very sensual, moment. Dax had called her a dozen times that week, on both her work and private lines. She'd had her assistant take a message, or let it go to voice mail, as her week had been too busy to get caught up in another one of the "projects" he always seemed to have on the back burner. Usually she didn't mind his enthusiasm. She'd enjoyed working on his campaign. But it seemed that the more time she devoted to his causes, the more he expected from her.

"I was beginning to worry when you didn't get back to me," he said, all but ignoring Roman, who she could see was not at all happy with the rude interruption. And neither was she. Normally she would have risen and greeted Dax with a platonic hug, or air-kissed him on each cheek, but this time she stayed put.

But he was being a typical self-centered, pushy politician, she supposed.

"I've been very busy," she told Dax, her irritation growing as he placed a heavy hand on her bare shoulder and gave it a squeeze.

"I have some ideas I need to run past you for an event I'd like to sponsor."

"This is a very busy time for me," she said, hoping to brush him off. "Call my assistant. Maybe she can squeeze you in after the holidays."

His smile never faltered. "I have a better idea. We'll meet for dinner tomorrow night. I'll pick you up at seven."

Was he asking her or telling her? Either way, the answer was no. "I'm busy tomorrow."

He wasn't swayed. "All right, Sunday, then."

What the hell was wrong with Dax? He was almost acting as if they were an item. Or as if he was deliberately trying to piss off Roman, and sabotage their evening. And Roman was seriously pissed off. His jaw was tense, and she could see that he wanted to interject. He glanced at her questioningly and she shot him a look that she hoped said, *let me handle it.*

Turning to Dax, she was firm, but polite. "Dax, I don't mean to be rude, but I just want to have a quiet evening with a friend. Call my assistant and I'll see what I can do."

He gave her shoulder another firm squeeze and she fought the urge to shrug his hand off, or bat it away. It wasn't like him to be so forward. Not with her anyway. Maybe Roman was right and Dax had set his sights on her. But she wasn't interested. Not even the least little bit. Sure, they had seen each other socially a few times, and had worked together, but she had never led him to believe she had any romantic intentions. If that's what he thought, he couldn't have been more mistaken.

"We'll talk next week," he said. He didn't ask,

he all but demanded. And she didn't justify it with a response. She just wanted him to leave.

When he finally removed his hand, the ghost of his touch made her feel so…icky. And he walked off having never even acknowledged that Roman was there.

So much for his respect for a *true* war hero.

"I'm so sorry, Roman. I'm not sure why Dax just did that. If I didn't know better I would say that he was jealous. Or trying to make you jealous."

"You know what I think," he said, sounding irritated.

She did, and she was beginning to believe he was right. "If he's looking for something beyond a professional relationship, I'm not interested. And if he thinks that kind of behavior is appropriate in any way, he had better start looking for a new volunteer."

"Good," Roman said, sounding relieved. "I don't trust him."

Right now, neither did she. "I could see that you wanted to say something to him."

"Oh, you have no idea," Roman said. "Let's just say that he's lucky he left when he did."

"Well, thank you for letting me handle it."

"I didn't feel like it was my place," he said. "As your friend."

She could swear he almost sounded hurt. Or disappointed. They had agreed to this arrangement. Did this mean he wanted more? Or was she just imagining things?

And if he did want more, how did she feel about that? Maybe she wanted more, too, if she could shake off her apprehension? He had been nothing but honest and up front with her, and had never made any excuses for his betrayal seven years ago. And she now truly believed that he had nothing to do with the recent slurs against her family. He was a good man, and a good friend. So why was she clinging so firmly to that last shred of resentment?

Just let it go and enjoy the night, and what you do have together, she told herself. *Don't overthink it. Keep it simple.*

"I don't want this to ruin our evening," she said.

"Neither do I."

She lowered her voice and added, "Just so we're clear, the only one getting into my panties is *you*." She paused, then said, "Though that could be a problem tonight."

"And why is that?"

She leaned forward, flashing him a sexy grin. "Because I'm not wearing any."

Nine

Roman was pretty sure Grace was kidding when she made the crack about not wearing panties. She was using it as a way to dispel the tension of the senator's rude interruption. Whether it was true or not, it worked.

Dax could have potentially ruined their evening, but Gracie didn't let that happen. She seemed just as disgusted by the senator's unnecessary intrusion as Roman was. And she finally seemed to be seeing the man for who he really was: a narcissistic, manipulative creep who had more on his mind than campaigns and fund-raising. After his stunt last Friday at the fund-raiser, Roman didn't want him within a hundred yards of Gracie.

He hoped she meant what she said and this would be the push she needed to stop working with Dax altogether. Roman had done a little digging, and asked around, and though he hadn't found anything outwardly corrupt in the senator's dealings, the general consensus seemed to be that the man was as crooked as they come—just very good at hiding it.

And though Roman tried not to let it show, he was jealous. When the senator put his hand on Gracie's shoulder Roman had caught himself clenching his fists. He didn't condone violence, but if they hadn't been in a crowded restaurant, his natural instinct to protect her would have left the senator with a broken hand.

But he'd let it go and they were able to eat and talk and enjoy each other's company the way they used to. He wanted to reach across the table and hold her hand, but he had to settle for a discreet game of footsie. But she took it a step further when she nudged out of her shoe and slid her foot up his leg. He nearly choked on his lobster when she slid her foot up his thigh and used her toes to play around in his crotch. He shot her a look, and she'd replied with a wicked grin. She was playing with fire and loving the hell out of it. Which only turned him on more. He slipped his hand under the table and stroked the arch of her foot and a fire lit in her eyes.

By the time they finished dinner, and the waiter asked if they wanted dessert, the only thing he had a taste for was her. He paid the bill and they waited impatiently as the valet brought the car around. Her back was to the valet stand, and there was no one around, so he reached up under her coat and copped a quick feel for a panty line, but couldn't find one. She smiled up at him and said, "Told ya."

When they were in the car, she took his hand and guided it under her dress.

Nope, definitely no panties that he could feel. Just soft, smooth skin, and she was already moist with arousal.

He cursed under his breath, his crotch tight.

"Are you as turned on as I am?" she asked.

"You tell me," he said taking her hand and guiding it to his zipper, hissing out a breath as she stroked him through his slacks.

"Drive," she said. "Fast."

She didn't have to tell him twice.

If it hadn't been for the fact that he had to shift gears, he would have kept his hand between her legs, but he tried to behave. Her, not so much. She leaned over and kissed him and he got so carried away the car behind him had to honk to get his attention when the light turned green.

Her place was closer by a good twenty minutes so he drove there. And rather than wait for the elevator, they took the stairs up to her fourth-floor loft. With her spiked heels slowing her down he got impatient at the second-floor landing. So he lifted her up, tossed her over his shoulder and carried her the rest of the way. It must have been a huge turn-on because they barely made it through the door before she shoved his coat down his arms and tugged at his belt. She unfastened his pants, shoved him against the door and dropped to her knees right there in the foyer. He groaned as she took him deep into her mouth, but he was so fired up he couldn't stand it for more than a minute or two before he had to stop her. Taking his own pleasure before hers was not, and never had been, an option.

When they made it to the bedroom she pulled her dress off and he discovered that not only was she not wearing panties, she didn't have a bra on, either. Just a pair of silky thigh-high stockings. Black, his personal favorite. With her tousled hair and flushed skin she looked like something out of a sexual fantasy. He had planned to make love to her, slow and sweet, but that clearly wasn't going to happen. Not this time.

So instead he shed the rest of his clothes, picked her up and tossed her onto the bed. She tried to pull him down on top of her, but he pinned her arms at her sides and buried his face between her thighs. She gasped and arched upward, curling her fingers into the covers. She was sweeter and more delicious than anything on the menu at the restaurant. And she was so turned on it couldn't have been thirty seconds before she moaned and shuddered and thrust her hips up as she shattered. She barely had time to catch her breath before she was up on her knees, pushing him onto his back.

He was hoping to take things a little bit slower but she was a woman on a mission. There was no stopping Gracie as she climbed on top of him, taking him deep inside of her. And it felt so damned good he didn't want to stop her. She was so hot and wet he had to dig extra deep to find the will and the control not to lose it instantly.

Head back, eyes closed, lost in her own world, she rode him hard and fast, bracing her hands on his chest, digging her nails into his skin. He gripped her hips, tried to slow her down, but it was already too late. He could feel the coil of pleasure pull tight in his groin, until it was almost too much to take, then let go in a hot rush.

He rode out the storm, and when he opened his eyes Gracie was smiling down at him. And all he could say was "Wow."

She laughed. "I'll take that as a compliment."

"Did you make it in time?"

She smiled and nodded.

"I tried to hold back."

"I know you did, and seeing you lose control made me lose control." She settled down on his chest, her skin hot against his. "That was incredible."

Yes, it was. But every time with her, no matter how they did it, was incredible. Fast, slow, he didn't care. As long as he was close to her. "I didn't really do much."

"Sometimes it's okay to just lie there and enjoy it," she said. "Let me do all the work."

He could live with that. "Well, it was the perfect end to a perfect evening."

Her laugh was a wry one. "Oh, but we're not done. Not even close. In fact…"

She got that devilish gleam in her eye, the one that said she was up to something. "I'll be right back," she told him, jumping off the bed and bolting from the room, then called over her shoulder, "Don't go anywhere."

Yeah, right. Like he had the energy to move. He could barely *breathe*.

He closed his eyes, trying not to fall asleep. He hadn't done any of the work, so why was he so wiped out?

"I'm back," she said several seconds later.

He opened his eyes and lifted his head.

She stood in the doorway, naked and flushed and sexy as hell, those damned thigh highs hugging her perfect legs just right. Holding a bottle of chocolate syrup in one hand and a can of whipped cream in the other, she grinned as she said, "How about a little dessert?"

The following Monday, Gracie sat at her drawing table in her studio, trying to sketch out a few pieces for next year's fall line, but she couldn't concentrate. Typically the view of the Chicago skyline out the long stretch of floor-to-ceiling windows was all she needed to inspire her, but it wasn't working today.

Today, she couldn't keep her mind off Roman.

He was all she seemed to think about lately. And not the way a friend should be thinking about another friend. Her feelings for him seemed to be spiraling out of control, and as much as it scared her, she'd never felt so alive and happy in her life. Or more conflicted. Why is it the two always seemed to go hand in hand?

Hard as she tried to stick to the friends-with-benefits arrangement, her heart would have no part of it. And she'd gone and done exactly what she promised herself she wouldn't do. She'd started to fall in love with him again. And she was pretty sure, knowing Roman the way she did, that he was falling for her, too.

It wasn't logical. It wasn't even sane. And to call it complicated didn't adequately describe what they would be getting themselves into if they took the next step.

A knock on her studio door had her looking up from her half-finished sketch. When the door opened and her sister Eve popped her head in, Gracie smiled.

"You busy?" Eve asked.

"Actually your timing is perfect," Gracie said,

tossing her pencil onto her drawing table. "I could use a break."

Eve crossed the room to look over Gracie's shoulder at the sketch she'd been trying to complete. "Nice."

"Thanks."

"It still blows me away at times how talented you are. You definitely got all the artistic talent in the family. I still draw like a third grader."

"What brings you to my side of town?" Gracie asked.

"Oh, I just thought I would stop in and say hi."

Gracie frowned. Eve was a very busy woman. She never just stopped in. If she went out of her way to drop by, she had a good reason to be there.

"Is everything okay with Sutton?"

"I talked to his nurse earlier and she said he's having a rough day, but he's stable."

"So what is it?"

"What is what?" Eve asked, going for a nonchalant look and failing miserably. "Can't I pay a visit to my baby sister?"

"Nope. You pretty much always have a reason. You might as well just tell me what it is." Though she was pretty sure she already knew what was bothering her sister.

"I'm worried about you, Grace."

"Worried about what?"

"You and Roman."

"Roman and I are friends."

"He almost ruined us."

"It was a long time ago, and he had nothing to do with the recent accusations. That was all Brooks."

"So what you're saying is, you trust him?"

"I do," she said.

Her sister eyed her cautiously. "Completely."

"Yes," Grace said, with not even a hint of reservation, and realized it was true. She really did trust him.

"Are you in love with him?"

Again there was no hesitation in her reply. "Yes, I'm in love with him."

Eve's troubled look didn't bode well, so Grace tried to explain.

"I know it probably doesn't make much sense to you. Hell, it doesn't make much sense to me, either. All I know is that everything inside me is screaming that he and I are supposed to be together. And though he's never come right out and said it, I think he feels the same way. We're just so...*good* together. I don't know how else to explain it. Even knowing that it could cause discord in the family, I still want him. And need him."

"I want you to be happy, Grace. We all do. And though I do have my reservations about Roman, I trust *you*, and I think that over time, after he proves himself, we'll learn to trust Roman, too. I just don't want to see you get hurt again."

"It's a chance I'm willing to take."

Eve took a deep breath and nodded, looking relieved. "Good. I guess I needed to hear that from you. I needed to see how sure you are. Because if you were still having reservations I had every intention of talking you out of seeing him, before you got in over your head."

Honestly she was already in over her head that first day in Sutton's office.

"There is something else I wanted to talk about," Eve said. "Daddy and I spoke last night and he's made the decision to change his will to include Carson."

Carson may have been a Newport, but he was just as much a Winchester. He was their brother, which gave him just as much right to the Winchester fortune as her and her sisters. The actions of his parents were in no way his fault, and as such it would be wrong to hold that against him.

"It's the right thing to do," Grace said.

Eve smiled and nodded. "I figured you would say that. I had my reservations at first, but I think you're right."

"How does Nora feel?" she asked, though Gracie was sure she already knew. Nora cared deeply about people, and had never taken any interest in money or power.

"She feels the way you do. I guess I was the only holdout. But he is our brother. Our blood. My only concern was that Brooks would use him to get what he wants, but now that I've gotten to know Carson I don't think that will happen. Graham said that Sutton's willingness to help them find their father, and the kindness he showed Cynthia in her time of need, has Brooks rethinking his priorities, and letting go of the bitterness."

"I know it's our legacy, and we should honor that, but in the end, it's only money."

"Guess we'll just have to hang in there and see what the future brings," Eve said.

Though her future was still hazy, one thing Gracie knew for sure was that hers would be a happy one.

In the world of private investigation, after months of dead ends there was nothing more satisfying than solving a case. And thanks to Sutton and his burst of conscience, less than a week after their meeting with the Newport boys, Roman now knew the identity of Graham and Brooks's father.

And the only thing more satisfying than solving the case was delivering the good news to the client.

Roman arranged a meeting for Wednesday morning, telling the brothers that he had information, and nothing more. This was news he wanted to deliver in person.

As he'd expected, the men showed up right on time. Roman's secretary showed them into the conference room at exactly 10:00 a.m. They walked in together looking anxious, and not at all as though they wanted to kill each other this time. Roman suspected that learning the truth about their mother had reminded them of the common ground they shared, and they had begun to repair their relationship. According to Gracie, who had talked to her sister Eve, Brooks had been very humbled by the truth and had begun to reevaluate his priorities, and his opinion of the man who'd essentially saved his mother's life.

Roman rose from his chair at the head of the table and shook both men's hands before he said, "Have a seat, gentlemen. Can I interest either of you in a beverage? Coffee? Water?"

The brothers declined with a shake of their heads, and rather than sitting on opposite sides of the table, sat side by side.

"So, you said you have information," Brooks said. "What do you know?"

Roman slid the file across his desk. "Your father's name is Beau Preston. He owns a horse ranch in Texas called the Lookaway."

"That was fast," Brooks said, looking as if he thought it was too good to be true. He opened the file so he and his brother could both read it.

"Cool Springs, Texas, is not a big place," Roman told them. "Once we knew where to look, and what to look for, the information was right there. It took some time, though, because the town doesn't even have a website."

"There isn't much here," Graham said.

"Unfortunately the town hasn't yet progressed into the digital age, so details are hard to come by. I wasn't sure how deep you wanted me to dig. I can get you more, but I'll have to send someone there, and in a town that small it won't be a covert operation. If there's a stranger there asking questions, word will probably spread fast. I wasn't sure if that's the way you want this to go down. Do you want your father to learn about you from the grapevine, or from his sons?"

Graham turned to his brother. "It's up to you, Brooks. This is your obsession."

"Are you saying you don't want to know?"

"No, I'm saying that this means more to you than it does to me. Do I want to know more? Absolutely. But I think that he should hear the truth from you or me, and not as gossip. And knowing how much this means to you, I think you should be the one to go."

The cocky real estate mogul looked more like a confused little boy. "To be honest, I'm not sure what I want to do. I've waited so long for this, and now it all seems to be moving so fast."

"Maybe you're just afraid of the truth," Graham said. "If this man knows nothing about us, he might not be thrilled to know that he has two illegitimate sons. We honestly have no idea how he'll react. Personally I need a little time to prepare myself for whatever happens. Good or bad."

Brooks's confusion couldn't be more obvious. "I've been so focused on finding him, I guess I haven't given much thought to the next step. Or considered that he might not want to see us."

"Take some time to think about it," Roman told him. "Beau Preston has lived in Cool Springs his entire life, and he owns a lucrative business. As a horse breeder he's well-known for his champion bloodlines. I doubt he's going anywhere."

"I think this is something that my brother and I should discuss in private," Graham said, rising from his seat to shake Roman's hand. "Thank you for not giving up on this and solving the case. It means so much to us."

"Don't thank me. If it hadn't been for Sutton, I would still be spinning my wheels."

Looking shell-shocked, Brooks rose and shook Roman's hand. Maybe this would bring him some peace, and he would finally be able to let go of the irrational anger and hatred he'd held for the Winchester family. With Brooks it was hard to say.

Now that he and Gracie were exploring a relationship, Roman was happy to put the whole matter to rest, before he found himself sucked into the middle of another scandal. Because he knew that Brooks, despite his humbled state, could turn on a dime with a renewed thirst for revenge. Roman supposed that all they could do was wait, and time would tell.

"Will I see you at the wedding next Thursday?" Graham asked him.

"Wedding?" Roman said, unsure of what he was referring to. Next Thursday was Thanksgiving, but he and Gracie hadn't yet discussed spending it together.

"Nora and Reid's," Graham said. "I just assumed, since you and Gracie…" He paused and said, "I'm sorry, did I speak out of turn?"

If Gracie wanted him there, she hadn't said so. She still needed time, and he understood that. It was a slow process gaining back her trust. But it would happen. Because as far as he was concerned, they were meant to be together.

"Don't apologize. What Gracie and I have is very…complicated."

After the men left, Roman sat there for several minutes thinking about his relationship with Gracie, and that maybe they needed to have a talk. He was in no hurry. He was fine with letting their relationship progress naturally. Maybe he just needed to know that they did have a future together.

They had spent the entire weekend together, and even carved out time for lunch together yesterday. He'd met her at her office and she had introduced him around to the junior designers on her staff. He didn't know a whole lot about the fashion industry, but he was impressed with what he saw, and her employees seemed to have the utmost respect for her. And from the looks of it, she was wildly successful. But he always knew that she would be.

He considered calling her just to say hi, then changed his mind. She was probably busy, and he had meetings to prepare for. They would talk later that evening. They did every night. Usually for an hour or more. And they were usually both still at work wrapping things up for the night. Like him, she was a workaholic, and typically hung around the office long after her employees went home for the night. Though he was sure that he would work less and delegate more if he had something, or better yet *someone*, to come home to.

As Roman was leaving the conference room, his secretary, Lisa, stopped him in the hallway.

"You got a call while you were in the meeting," she said.

"From who?"

"A Special Agent Crosswell, from the FBI."

Roman frowned. *The FBI?* What could they possibly want from him? "Did he say what he was calling for?"

"No, but he asked that you get back to him right away. He said it was an urgent matter. I left his contact information on his desk."

"Thanks, Lisa."

She eyed him quizzically. "Anything I should know about, boss?"

"I'll let you know as soon as I do."

She smiled. "Fair enough. I'm leaving to run some errands and pick up lunch. Would you like me to bring you back something?"

He was too distracted now to eat. "No, thanks."

He went to his corner office. He'd bought the company from a college friend who after a decade in the business decided the life of a PI wasn't for him. What had started as a three-office, four-employee operation was now a thriving business in a swanky downtown location. The agency took up an entire floor of the building and he now employed over three dozen people. And he still couldn't keep up with all the business coming his way. Unless things slowed down, he would have to look into expanding again. It was as if everything that he'd ever wanted in life was being dropped at his feet.

Well, almost everything. With Gracie it was a little more complicated.

He called the number Lisa left him and got the agent's voice mail. Annoyed and curious as to what he wanted, he left a message, then sat back to wait for a return call, going over a list of potential new clients.

Not five minutes later, the agent called back, and as he answered Roman felt an unusual sense of apprehension. "Roman Slater."

"Mr. Slater, my name is Rudy Crosswell. I'm a special agent with the FBI's fraud division. I was hoping you would be willing to meet with me this afternoon."

Well, you didn't get much more direct than that. "In regard to...?"

"I'd rather speak to you in person. Could we set something up?"

"Am I being investigated? Should I have counsel?"

"No, sir, nothing like that," he assured Roman. "The truth is, we need your help."

Well, that was good to know. His afternoon was booked, but this being the FBI, he felt it took precedence. "Can you be here at four?"

"Actually I was hoping you could come to the field office. It's a matter of the utmost secrecy."

Now Roman was really intrigued. "I'll work it in."

They decided on a time and when Lisa returned two hours later Roman asked her to cancel everything on his schedule for the afternoon. When he arrived at the field office Agent Crosswell met him in the lobby at the metal detector. The man was middle-aged, and looked to be ex-military with a graying buzz cut and serious eyes. Roman had to surrender the firearm he always kept strapped to his ankle and the knife from his inside coat pocket. Then the agent handed him a guest badge and led

Roman through an open area crammed with cubicles and bustling with activity to his office in the back. The fact that he had an office said that he was fairly far up the ranks.

Roman's suspicion that he was military was confirmed when he saw the medals displayed in the agent's office, including a Medal of Honor and a Purple Heart. Otherwise the room was small, plain and a little outdated with its '90s-era furniture.

"Please have a seat," he told Roman.

Roman sat in one of two uncomfortable-looking chairs. "When did you serve?"

"Gulf War," he said, sitting at his desk, which was as clean and organized as the rest of the room. Another military trait. "I'll get right to the point. And what I'm about to tell you doesn't go past this office."

"Of course."

"I'm heading up a task force investigating political corruption on the state level. I need someone to do some outside digging."

"On who?"

"Dax Caufield."

Son of a bitch. Roman knew there was something not quite right about the senator, which made Gracie's affiliation with him that much more disturbing. "You think he's corrupt."

"I *know* he's corrupt. I just can't prove it yet. Two months into office it was rumored that he was tak-

ing bribes from business lobbyists in exchange for
his support on key legislation. But he's smart, and
hasn't left a paper trail. The case is weak at best.
We're fairly sure we can get him on misuse of campaign funds, though. And that's where you come in."

Roman didn't like where this was going. "Why
me?"

"Considering your past experience with political
corruption, and your current connections, you're the
perfect man for the job."

"What connections would those be?" he asked,
afraid he already knew the answer.

"Grace Winchester."

Ten

Shit. This was the last thing Roman needed. He rose from his seat, which was just as uncomfortable as it looked, and told Agent Crosswell, "I'm sorry, but I can't help you."

The agent leaned back in his chair, nonplussed. "You may want to rethink that."

"Why?"

"Because as far as we know, she could be involved. She could be hiding evidence."

No way. Knowing Grace the way he did, Roman didn't believe that for a second. Besides, he'd gone down this road before and he'd lost the only thing that mattered to him. He would not take that chance again. "She would never do that. If she does have evidence, I'm betting she doesn't know it."

"An undercover operative learned from a source that she may be in possession of files that would prove the misappropriation of funds and even the bribery we suspect him of."

If they had undercover people working this, it was clearly a serious investigation. He didn't want to see Gracie implicated. She had been through enough in the past few months. "I can tell you right now that she isn't hiding anything. She worked on his campaign because she believed in his politics. She would never knowingly hide evidence. Going after her would be a waste of your time."

"She may not know that she has the evidence, but we've learned that the senator thinks she does and that she may know something she shouldn't. If she isn't working in collusion with Senator Caufield—and that's the theory we're leaning toward—our concern is that he will do anything to get them back from her, and keep her quiet if necessary. Meaning that she could be in serious danger."

The idea of Gracie getting hurt made his heart beat faster. If she truly was in danger he had to listen to what Agent Crosswell had to say.

Roman reclaimed his seat. "You're sure about this."

Crosswell nodded. "Without a doubt."

"What do you need from me?"

"We need to get to those files before the senator can. Do you have any idea where they might be located?"

With a shrug, Roman said, "Not a clue, but I can ask her."

"No. Absolutely not. If she suddenly drops out of sight, Senator Caufield will know something is up. We can't take the chance of the investigation going public. We have too many man-hours invested in this to blow it. The senator cannot know that we're investigating him. Whatever you have to do, Miss Winchester cannot know about it."

"And if I tell her?"

"I can charge you with impeding a federal investigation."

Great. It was his past coming back to bite him in the ass. If Gracie was truly in danger his first instinct was to take her as far from Chicago as he could, if that's what it took to keep her safe. But there was no way Gracie would agree to that. Not without knowing why.

Dax had obviously had Gracie completely snowed. Then Roman thought of something that nearly made his heart stop altogether. "The senator has been trying to set up a meeting with her."

"We know. You can't let that meeting happen. If she gives him the files, our investigation is over. Or worse, she could be charged as an accomplice."

Jesus, how did he keep getting into these impossible situations? "This is emotional blackmail."

"I know. And I'm not unsympathetic."

His sympathy wouldn't stop his and Gracie's relationship from crashing and burning. "I can't lie to her."

The agent leaned forward, his expression serious. "Mr. Slater, if it's her life on the line, can you afford not to?"

Gracie came home from work early after a surprise call from Roman that afternoon. Though they typically didn't see each other on weeknights, he'd said he missed her and offered to bring dinner over. The truth was, she missed him, too, and seeing him only on the weekends just wasn't cutting it anymore. And it would give them an opportunity to talk about their relationship.

There was no question in her mind that she loved him, and she wanted them to be together. And she was fairly certain that he wanted the same thing if it felt as right to him as it did to her.

She had just gotten out of the shower and was still wrapped in a towel when her sister Nora called. With her wedding barely a week away she was scrambling to make last-minute preparations. Normally Gracie would have helped with the arrangements but she had just been too busy with work, and the proposed date had been too close for Gracie to arrange for time off. But Nora, sweet as she was, had been understanding.

"Reid and I took Declan for the final fitting on the tuxes," Nora told her. "He looks so adorable."

Declan, Nora's son from her first marriage, was a precocious two-year-old with curly ginger hair, adorable freckles and striking blue eyes. Nora's fiancé hadn't been open to taking on another man's child at first, which had worried Gracie and Eve, and especially Sutton. But Reid proved himself to be an amazing father and the three couldn't be happier.

"I wish there was something I could do to help," Gracie told her. "I know you have your hands full."

"I'm fine. For once in your life I want you to just enjoy a family event instead of feeling like you have to run it."

But that was what Gracie did. She helped people. She sacrificed her own time to make the lives of others easier. "Well, if there's anything you need me to do—"

"There isn't," Nora insisted. "You are a guest at this wedding and I want you to act like one. Which reminds me, are you planning to bring a date? I'd like to have the final list ready by tomorrow. And I've heard a thing or two…"

Of course she was talking about Roman.

"Would it be a problem if I brought someone?"

"Honey, of course not."

Gracie frowned. Maybe she just didn't understand who Gracie would be bringing. "Seriously, I can bring *anyone*?"

Nora laughed. "Why are you beating around the bush? If you want to bring Roman that's fine. I think it's better than fine."

Huh? "You do? After what he did to our family…"

"That was a long time ago, and Eve explained that he had nothing to do with this last scandal. He's human, Grace. Everyone makes mistakes. Everyone deserves a second chance. And it's obvious that he makes you happy. There's a light in your eyes that I haven't seen in ages. I'm not saying that he doesn't have to prove himself, but I do think he has potential."

Her relief at hearing that left her weak in the knees. "I'm in love with him again."

"Again?"

What was her sister implying? That Gracie hadn't really been in love with Roman before? "I'm not sure what you mean."

"I'm curious, Grace. How many men have you dated seriously in the past seven years? Just a rough number."

Nora already knew the answer to that. Gracie had used work and her charity obligations as an excuse to avoid dating, but the truth was, no man had come along whom she'd been interested in dating more than once or twice. She always compared them to Roman.

"None," she told her sister.

"Exactly."

She wasn't sure what her sister was trying to say. "Meaning what?"

"Is it possible that maybe you never *stopped* loving him?"

Leave it to Nora to speak her mind and tell it like it was. And of course Gracie had considered that. "At this point, I'm not really sure. I just know that I feel good when I'm with him. We just…fit. The thought of letting him back in then losing him again terrifies me. Maybe it's not so much that I don't trust him. Maybe I don't trust myself."

"I know all about loss, honey, believe me. When I lost Sean I thought I would never recover."

Nora's husband and childhood sweetheart, Sean O'Malley, had died fighting in the war in Iraq. He'd given his life saving other soldiers. Gracie hadn't forgotten how devastated Nora had been to lose the love of her life. The only thing that had kept her going was her son, Declan. And she'd sworn that she would never give her heart to a man again. But here she was, now happily engaged, deeply in love and about to get married. People did get second chances.

Maybe it was now meant to be, and seven years ago just hadn't been their time.

"Your only other option is to not try," Nora said. "Is that what you want?"

No, not trying wasn't an option at all. They had something good. Something special. "I can barely imagine my life without him in it. I've never been able to talk to anyone the way I can talk to him. He accepts me for who I am. He sees past the Winchester name and appreciates me for *me*. He always has. In a couple of weeks he's gone from being my mortal enemy to my best friend. How do you give up on something like that?"

"Simple. You don't. You give it your all, and you fight for what you want. And you don't stop until you have no fight left in you."

Nora was right. Gracie needed to fight for them. And the truth was that so far, she hadn't even had to fight all that hard. Everything just seemed to be falling into place. It was almost too easy. But easy was good, and she planned to enjoy it.

"Yes," she told her sister. "I'm bringing Roman to the wedding."

Nora sounded genuinely pleased when she said, "Wonderful! I'm so happy for you, Grace."

Her doorbell rang. "Speak of the devil. Roman is here. I have to go."

"If I don't talk to you before then, I'll see you next Thursday. Love you!"

"Love you, too!" Gracie hung up, slipped a robe on and scurried to the door. Roman was early. He wasn't supposed to be there for another half an hour, but she didn't care. She couldn't wait to see him.

She pulled the door open, ready to throw herself

into his arms, and was surprised to find not Roman standing there, but Dax Caufield.

Before Gracie could say a word, Dax walked right in without invitation, and for a second she was too stunned to say or do anything. He'd been blowing up her phone and nagging her assistant since Friday, after Gracie had seen him at the restaurant. But to show up uninvited at her home?

"Dax, what are you doing here? And how did you get in?"

He avoided her question entirely. With a smile that didn't quite reach his eyes, he shrugged out of his coat and said, "You've been avoiding me, Grace."

She instinctively pulled her robe tighter around herself. She'd always felt comfortable with Dax. He'd been to her place a dozen times before when they'd worked on the campaign and she'd never thought twice about it. But something about this surprise visit, and the vibe she was getting from him, felt very wrong. She made a mental note to have a serious talk with her doorman. She didn't care if it was the president there to see her, he should have called up. "As I told you the other night, I've been very busy."

He took a seat on the couch, making himself comfortable. "You don't look busy now. Let's talk."

Who the hell was he to tell her if she was or wasn't busy? Why was he acting like this? "This is not a good night for me."

"I won't take too much of your time," he said. "I promise."

He already had taken too much time. And he was making her uncomfortable. She didn't like the way he was looking at her, and the fact that all she had on was a thin silk robe.

"You could offer me a drink," he said, crossing one leg over the other, settling back as if he was planning to stay a while.

He was trying to intimidate her, she realized. He was bullying her. She'd seen him do it before, never to her but to his political enemies during the campaign. She hadn't cared for it then, and she really didn't like it now.

"Dax, I'm going to have to ask you to leave."

With a sigh he leaned forward, clasping his hands together. "Grace, I can't do that."

She went from uncomfortable to downright uneasy. He was actually refusing to leave her home?

"Grace, I have a problem and I need your help."

"What kind of problem?"

"There are people out to get me. They're trying to ruin me, Grace."

Well, of course there were. He was a politician and it was a cutthroat business. And what did he think she could do about it? "Who is trying to ruin you?"

"People who don't like my politics. Who think there's no place for a straight shooter in the senate.

They tried to buy my vote, and when I refused they set out to ruin me."

Unless he had something to hide, it shouldn't have mattered who was after him. "How can they do that if you've done nothing wrong?"

"That's why I need all the files you have from the campaign. It's the only way to prove my innocence."

That made no sense. "You have copies of everything."

"You're going to have to trust me on this, Grace. I need you to hand over everything you have."

That was the problem, wasn't it? She *didn't* trust him. Not anymore. He wasn't acting like himself, and it was scaring her a little. "Dax, I'm sorry, but I don't have backups of anything."

"Grace," he said, rising from the couch. "We both know that's not true."

She took a step back, not just intimidated, but actually scared. "Dax, you have to leave right now."

He took a step toward her. Casually, but there was a darkness in his eyes that made her heart beat faster and her breath hitch.

"I really need your cooperation. It's a simple request."

She held her ground, but her knees had started to knock. "I can't give you something I don't have."

"We can do this now. You can hand over the flash drive and we can be done with it, or I can send someone to get it for me. And my colleagues are not as patient as I am. It's up to you, Grace."

Colleagues? He was threatening to send someone to do what? Rough her up?

Who the hell was this man?

"If you don't leave now I'm going to call the police," she told him, squaring her shoulders, struggling to hide the tremble in her voice, wishing she had her cell phone. If she could record his threats…

"That's not advisable, Grace. You would be wise to cooperate."

Screw that, and screw him. With a surge of courage that came from somewhere deep inside of her, she walked past Dax and grabbed the cordless phone off the coffee table. She punched in 911, and with her finger hovering over the button to connect the call, said firmly, *"Get. Out."*

Dax shrugged and shook his head, as if he were disappointed in her, then grabbed his coat. "Don't say I didn't warn you."

He strolled to the door, casually pulling his coat on, and without looking back, walked out. She ran to the door and locked it behind him. That was when the reality of what had just happened hit her full force, and she started to shake from the inside out. What could ever possess Dax to treat her that way? To bully and threaten her.

She felt betrayed and used and so stupid for not seeing sooner what he was really like.

And why were her copies of the files so critical? They were no different from his. At least, they shouldn't be.

Something was up, and she had the feeling that it had nothing to do with his innocence. If people were out to get him there must be a damned good reason. And she wanted to know why.

She collapsed onto the couch and sat there for several minutes, trying to calm down, stuck somewhere between grief and fear and hurt. The sharp rap on the door several minutes later nearly had her jumping out of her skin. Was that Dax's colleague already? Was he there to rough her up?

It took all her courage, but she got up and with shaky knees walked to the door, checking the peephole this time.

It was Roman. She went limp with relief. She threw the door open, hurled herself into his arms, knocking the bag of food he'd brought right out of his hand, and started to cry.

Eleven

"Gracie, what's wrong?" Roman asked, holding her tight, though he was pretty sure he already knew the answer.

She buried her face against his chest and sobbed, clinging to him like he was her lifeline, trembling all over.

He walked her backward into the apartment and shut the door behind them. When he'd pulled onto her street he had seen a man, one who'd looked an awful lot like Dax Caufield, leave her building and climb into a limo, but he'd been too far away to tell for sure.

Now he knew.

He wanted to know what had happened, if Dax had hurt her, but she was in no shape to explain.

So he held her tight until the sobs subsided and she stopped trembling.

"Are you okay?" he asked, holding her away from him and cradling her face in his hands so he could see her eyes, which were all red and puffy.

"I am now," she said, sniffing and wiping the tears from her cheeks. "Dax came by."

His heart skipped a beat. He should have gotten there sooner. He should have gone straight to her when he left the FBI. To protect her. But there had been no way to know Dax would be so bold as to show up at her apartment. "Tell me what happened."

She told him how Dax had arrived unannounced and harassed her, even threatened her, for the flash drive from his campaign. That he would flat out threaten someone of Grace's social standing disturbed Roman more than anything. Dax was either running scared and desperate and making mistakes, or so arrogant he thought he was invincible.

"Did you give him the flash drive?" he asked her.

"I told him I didn't have them."

"Do you?"

She nodded. "In my file cabinet. Something isn't right, Roman. He has the same copies of everything that I do. Why is this so important that he would threaten me? I thought he was a decent guy. How could I have been so wrong?"

"I'm sorry," he said. He didn't know what else to say. At this point there was nothing else he *could* say. He was bound to secrecy by the FBI. His hands were tied. "Maybe it would be better if I held on to them for you. Just to be safe."

She shook her head firmly. "I refuse to let him intimidate me. I'm going to go over every single one of the files and see what it is he's so anxious about."

That was not a good idea. Roman didn't know what was in the files and he didn't want to take a chance on her seeing something she shouldn't and putting herself in even more danger. "Maybe you shouldn't." And he couldn't even explain why he was saying that.

"Roman, I have to. I have to know what's going on."

He knew that once Gracie set her mind to something, changing it was next to impossible. But he couldn't let her do this alone. "Then would you at least let me look at them with you?"

She seemed relieved. "Of course. Maybe you'll see something I would have otherwise missed."

"Get dressed and pack a bag," he said.

She frowned. "Why am I packing a bag?"

"Because you're staying with me until we sort this out." There was no way he was taking a chance and leaving her alone. He had friends in the security business. If necessary he would hire someone to shadow her when he couldn't be there.

"I can't let him scare me out of my home. If I keep the door locked—"

"Gracie, the sort of people we're talking about

won't be stopped by a locked door. And they won't hesitate to hurt you if they don't get what they want."

Gracie looked so confused and hurt when she said, "I didn't even know that he had connections to people like that. Maybe he really doesn't, and he was just trying to scare me."

Roman seriously doubted it. He'd done a bit of digging and talked to a few people after his meeting with the FBI. Everyone agreed that while Dax had a stellar public persona, he also had a dark side, and reputed connections to some very bad people. Not just corrupt public officials and businessmen but the mob, as well. But no one as of yet had been able to prove it. "I'm not taking that chance," he told Gracie. Agent Crosswell had forbidden him from telling her about the investigation, but he couldn't stop Roman from protecting her. "Now pack some things. We're leaving."

Grace had only lasted an hour or so before the adrenaline rush of being threatened by a man she thought was her friend left her completely drained of energy. Roman had tucked her into his bed, then sat at his desk and got back to work. By 5:00 a.m., he had a pretty good idea of why the senator was so hot to get his hands on Grace's files. After comparing them to the documents on public record, there were major inconsistencies.

Until the senator got what he wanted, or the FBI

nailed Dax for his crimes, Gracie would continue to be in danger. And Roman would do anything necessary to keep her safe. Even if he had to do it covertly.

The only way to put an end to this was to hand over everything she had to the FBI. The quickest way would be to make copies of the flash drive, and Gracie would never be the wiser. But while he could view the information on his computer, the flash drive was locked with a code and couldn't be duplicated or altered in any way. The only way to prove the senator's guilt was to take the original flash drive and hand it over to Agent Crosswell. But Roman would have to do it behind Gracie's back. Meaning he would be forced to lie to her.

Just like before.

The realization had been like an arrow through his heart. This was supposed to be their second chance. But it was the only way to keep her safe.

"Good morning," he heard Gracie say, and looked up to find her standing in his office doorway, wrapped in a blanket, her hair tousled from sleep. "Have you been up all night?"

He nodded, wondering what the hell he was going to do next.

"Did you find anything?"

He'd given this a lot of thought, and he'd made a choice, one that could save Grace's—and his own—ass.

"Nothing," he told her. "I found nothing at all."

* * *

Confused, Grace said, "Nothing? Are you sure?"

"I'm sure."

She drew in a deep breath then blew it out. "Well, then, what was the big deal about him getting the flash drive?"

"I don't know, Gracie."

"Do you think I should just give them to him?"

"Hold off a while," Roman told her, looking as confused as she was. "There's clearly something shady going on and I want a little more time to dig. I'll keep the flash drive and you're going to stay here just in case."

"For how long?"

He got up and crossed the room to where she stood, putting his arms around her. "I wish I could answer that."

This was crazy. When and if she ever moved in with Roman, she wanted it to be the next step in their relationship, not some twisted obligation to keep her safe. It wasn't right. "I could stay at my father's estate. That place is like Fort Knox."

Roman tipped her chin up so he could look in her eyes. "Is that your way of saying you don't want to be here with me?"

"No, of course not. I just… I don't want to inconvenience you."

He dipped his head and kissed her gently, and

her heart melted on the spot. "You could never be an inconvenience to me, Gracie."

She laid her head on his chest and held on tight. "Maybe this is a bad time, but there's something I think we need to talk about."

"Something bad?"

"No, just something that's been on my mind."

"Can it wait till I take a shower?"

She stroked the side of his face with her palm. It was rough with beard stubble. "Of course. Would you like me to make you breakfast? Or did you want to get some sleep first?"

"No time for sleep," he said. "I'm used to pulling all-nighters so it's not a big deal. And I would love some breakfast. Give me fifteen minutes."

While Roman showered, Grace threw on her robe and headed to the kitchen. Considering he was a man, his refrigerator and cupboards were insanely well stocked with, for the most part, healthy foods. But he'd always taken good care of himself, exercising regularly and eating well. He did have his weaknesses, though, two being bacon and eggs.

She opened the fridge and found a slab of thick-sliced bacon, a half-empty carton of eggs and a jug of orange juice. From the pantry she pulled out a loaf of raisin bread, which had always been a favorite of his in the mornings. That she remembered his habits was a comfort somehow.

She found the pots and pans she needed and got to

work. She had skipped dinner last night, and though she didn't have much of an appetite now, she knew that she needed to eat. But it would be difficult with the huge knot twisting her insides. It was still a little surreal the way Dax had spoken to her, and threatened her. She'd thought for sure that Roman would find something incriminating in the files.

She had hoped she would wake up this morning and it would all make sense. Now she was more confused than ever. She was tempted to give Dax the flash drive and just be done with the whole thing, but intuition told her to wait and let Roman dig deeper. She trusted him, and she knew that if anyone could figure this out he could. And if she really was in some sort of danger, he would keep her safe. Despite all that they had been through she had never once doubted that he would sacrifice his own life to save hers.

There had been an incident back in college, when they were still just friends. They had been studying at the university library for finals and he was walking her back to her sorority house when a strung-out-looking guy, not much older than them, pulled a gun on them and demanded Gracie's purse and Roman's wallet. Without hesitation Roman had stepped in front of her. Whatever the guy had been on, his hands had been shaking and he'd been visibly agitated. Roman had spoken to him in a very calm and rational voice and done as he'd asked, handing over the requested items. As soon as the guy had them, he'd run off. He was never caught, and it had been a pain in the butt having to replace everything in her purse, but Roman's cool head and quick thinking had saved them from further trouble.

Still, she hated that she *needed* someone's protection. It was just all so confusing and disturbing, but she trusted Roman to do the right thing.

When he walked into the kitchen fifteen minutes later he was freshly showered, clean-shaven and dressed for work in black slacks and a black cashmere sweater, carrying a black blazer that he hung over the back of a chair at the kitchen table. "Something smells good," he said.

"Bacon, eggs sunny-side up, raisin toast and juice. And of course coffee." She had the feeling they were both going to need it. "Have a seat."

He took a spot at the table while she fixed their plates, and he asked, "What did you want to talk about?"

Here we go, she thought, and the knots that had begun to loosen in her belly cinched tight again. What if she poured her heart out to him, and he rejected her? What if to him this was just a fling? What if he was content being single and on the market?

But what if he wasn't?

She served the food and sat down, taking a deep

breath for courage. "The last few weeks have been wonderful," she said.

He nodded and smiled, but his eyes were serious. "I think so, too."

"Despite everything that's happened between us, I feel as if we've really reconnected."

"I feel that way, too."

She was so nervous the smell of the eggs was upsetting her stomach so she pushed her plate away. Why couldn't she just say it?

"Obviously something is on your mind that you're hesitant to talk about," he said. "Whatever it is, good or bad, I want you to tell me." He reached across the table and took her hand. "If that's what *you* want."

For a big tough guy he was so damned sweet sometimes.

She swallowed her fear, and her pride, and said, "I know we agreed on our friends-with-benefits arrangement, but everything feels different now. I feel different. But before I get in any deeper I need to know if you feel the same way. If you think we have a future together. I know it's only been a few weeks, and I don't want to rush you—"

"Yes."

She blinked. "Yes?"

"Yes," he said, still holding her hand, and the affection in his eyes was so nakedly honest her heart shifted in her chest. "I see us having a future together. I want us to be together. That's all I've ever wanted, Gracie. Hard as I tried to forget you, I never could. You're a part of me. I know there's bad feelings, and it will take time, but not being with you isn't an option anymore. We can just take it one day at a time."

She was so relieved, and so happy that she'd had the courage to ask.

"I can do that," she said. Hell, in the past she had waited two years for their relationship to bloom into something more than friendship.

"I do have one more question," she said. "What are you doing for Thanksgiving?"

"I was kind of hoping someone would invite me to Nora and Reid's wedding," he said with a grin.

His smile warmed her from the inside out. "Would you be my date?"

"I would love to," he said, pressing a kiss to the back of her hand, then letting go. "But right now I have to eat and get to work."

"This early?" she said, feeling disappointed. She had been hoping they might have a little time to fool around before he left.

"My day is booked solid. How about you?"

The truth was, she had more work than she could handle. They were obviously both workaholics, but she was sure they could make that work. "I'll probably shower and get to the office early, too."

"Not gonna happen."

"I have to go to work."

"And you will, but I'm sending a car for you. It will take you to and from work, or anywhere else you need to go. I don't want you going anywhere alone. Understand?"

"You don't think that's excessive?"

"Not at all. A threat is a threat."

"But if there's nothing on the flash drive—"

"This is not negotiable," he said firmly. "We're not taking any chances."

"Maybe I should take a look at that flash drive again and see if there's something you missed. I know that campaign like the back of my hand."

"Actually I was going to take them with me to work. I want to make a few inquiries and take another look at them. Besides, if the senator really is determined to get them, his 'associate' will never get past my building security. They'll be safest there."

"Should I maybe call the police? Like you said, a threat is a threat."

"They're going to want proof. I hate to say it, but it's your word against a state senator's, and you might not be taken seriously. He has connections. It might only make the situation worse."

Roman was probably right. Dax was extremely well liked. And well connected. "It's just so frustrating that he can get away with that. That he can threaten and bully me with no consequences. I did so much for him. I really believed in him. I feel so betrayed, and so stupid for not seeing who he really is."

"You could only see what he let you see. He's a politician, and sadly most of them will say or do anything to appeal to the base and get elected. And they'll do anything to avoid a scandal. This is why I stay away from clients with political motivations."

"I'm sorry you had to be dragged into this. I'm pretty sure this will be the last time I venture into the political realm."

Roman got up and put his plate in the sink, then shrugged into his blazer. "What time should I have the car pick you up?"

"You know, I could have one of my dad's limos take me where I need to go."

"Is his driver trained to kill a man with his bare hands?"

Boy, he really was serious about keeping her safe. "Um...well..."

"I didn't think so. So don't bother arguing, it will be a waste of time."

"How long do I have to live like this?"

"Hopefully not long. Let me make some calls today, and do some digging. I'll update you when I get home tonight. In the meantime I want you to talk to the security detail at your office. Let them know that there could be a problem, but don't go into any detail."

"What should I tell him exactly?"

"Just tell him that you've gotten threatening phone calls, and he needs to watch for anything suspicious."

"Okay," she said, the whole situation still feeling so surreal. Like something she would see on one of those true-crime shows.

"I have to go, but I'll call you later. And call me if you need anything."

She rose from her seat to kiss him goodbye. "I will, I promise. And thank you for everything."

"You don't have to thank me." He kissed her gently and stroked her cheek with the backs of his fingers. "I will move heaven and earth to keep you safe."

She smiled up at him. "I know. And I should be ready to leave by eight."

"I'll make sure the car is here by then. And *be careful*."

"I will. Have a good day." She almost said *I love you*. It was on the tip of her tongue, but she held it in. *One day at a time, take it slow, no pressure.*

Now that she knew where she stood, and that they were headed in the right direction, that was good enough for her. She trusted Roman with her life, and now she trusted him with her heart.

Twelve

As soon as Roman was in his car he called Agent Crosswell and left a message. The guilt of having to lie to Gracie was eating him alive. He loved her, he wanted to be with her for the rest of his life and this deception was killing him. But he couldn't risk her getting hurt or, almost as bad, going down as an accomplice. He'd come so close to telling her the truth, but he just couldn't. Hell, for all he knew the FBI could have his place bugged. It wasn't unheard of. And if this thing was going to end, he had to turn the flash drive over to them. He had no other choice. But before he did, before he would even take them to the FBI building, he and Agent Crosswell were going to sit down and talk, and put together some sort of deal to protect Gracie from any form of legal retribution or liability.

There was no doubt in Roman's mind that the senator had committed fraud, and Roman would not let Gracie get sucked into what had the potential to be an epic scandal. That was the last thing she needed. As a key player in the senator's campaign she would definitely feel some backlash. There was no way to avoid that. And at some point she would probably have to testify at trial, unless the senator took a deal. But Roman doubted he would. He was too arrogant to believe he would ever be found guilty. But this house of cards he'd built was about to come down.

Roman would insist that it be made clear, unequivocally and with no question, that Gracie was in no way involved in the senator's illegal dealings. Because it was often people in her position who went down as the fall guy. And the senator was just the sort of man to throw someone else under the bus to save his own ass and not think twice about it.

The more he learned about the man, the more troubling the situation became. Roman knew that Dax must have friends in high places, but he had learned the misconduct was further reaching than even he'd imagined. And as badly as he wanted to see the senator go down, his main priority was making sure Gracie walked away unscathed.

If Gracie wasn't given full immunity, the FBI would never see that flash drive.

When he got to work he made the car arrangements for Gracie, hiring a fully armed driver whom he spoke to personally. Knowing there would be someone to watch her back took his stress level down considerably. Then, at 8:30 a.m., Agent Crosswell called him back.

"We need to have a meeting," Roman told him.

"You have what I want?" he asked.

"We talk first."

There was a long pause, as if the agent were thinking it through, then he said, "Fair enough. One o'clock, my office."

"I'll be there," Roman said. The flash drive was already locked away in his office safe, and wouldn't be coming back out until he had everything that he needed from the FBI. And as soon as he was able, he would come clean with Gracie and hope she understood why he had to lie to her. That he was doing it to protect her. Because this time he had no doubt in his mind of her innocence. That he'd believed she could be guilty of anything seven years ago still haunted him. He'd betrayed her, and though he had moved on, the guilt had never completely gone away. But he would spend the rest of his life making it up to her if that was what it took. And he hoped that she could eventually forgive him. Until then he wasn't going to push. Like he told Gracie, one day at a time.

The meeting with the FBI went well, and Crosswell agreed to a deal giving Gracie full immunity.

Roman also insisted that her name be kept out of this for as long as humanly possible. Still, he knew that there would be no way to completely avoid the fall-out. They made arrangements for an agent to pick the flash drive up at his office later that afternoon, and of course he showed up right on time, dressed as a delivery man. Handing them over, knowing he was deceiving Gracie, was one of the hardest things Roman had ever had to do. But he just kept remind-ing himself that he was doing it for her safety. Be-cause when this blew open, it wasn't just Dax who would be going down. Some very prominent offi-cials would be shoved into the spotlight, not to men-tion local authorities and their mob connections. But if the FBI was going to make their case, he hoped they would do it soon, because as long as Dax sus-pected her of having that flash drive she would be in danger. Hell, even if she turned them over to him, and he suspected her of knowing the truth, he might do something drastic to silence her. Something that would surely look like an accident. Roman had seen it before. And he knew that the longer he had to lie to Gracie, the worse the damage would be when the truth came out.

Roman had a hell of a time concentrating the rest of the afternoon. He must have texted Mark, Gracie's driver/bodyguard, a dozen times to check up on them.

Mark, an ex-marine, finally had enough, and late in the afternoon, sent him a terse text:

Relax boss, I've got it.

Roman didn't make it home until almost eight, and the limo was still in the driveway, which alarmed him. The security system at his home was top-of-the-line, so he hadn't asked or expected Mark to stick around after she was home for the night, but when he walked into the house they were sitting at the kitchen table eating pizza. Gracie had a beer, and Mark, ever the professional, was drinking a bottle of soda. She had exchanged her work clothes for a pair of leggings and an oversize sweatshirt. With her hair pulled back in a ponytail, she looked just like she had back in college.

As soon as she saw him, Gracie smiled and stood to greet him. "Sorry we started without you, but I was starving."

He walked over to her and she threw her arms around his neck and kissed him. She tasted like tomato sauce and beer. "Did you have a good day?"

Hell no, not even close. "I had a busy day."

She shrugged and said, "I guess busy is good. I was just telling Mark that my new purse line is doing fantastic. They're flying off the shelves. We're going to make record profits this quarter."

"That's great," he said with a smile, wishing he could share her enthusiasm.

Mark finished his soda and stood. "I'm going to head out. What time tomorrow, ma'am?"

"Gracie," she said. "And let's say seven thirty if that's okay. I have an early meeting to prepare for."

"I'll be here."

"A word?" Roman asked Mark, who nodded. "I'll be right back," Roman said to Gracie over his shoulder as he left.

When they were outside, Mark said, "I hope you don't mind that I stayed. She offered pizza and I was hungry."

"I don't mind, I just saw the limo still here and thought the worst. So there was no trouble today? No sign of anyone following you?"

Mark shook his head. "Nothing. And I have to say, that's one hell of a great girl you've got there."

Roman couldn't suppress a smile. "She is."

"When you told me who she was I expected her to be snooty or arrogant. I was wrong. I told her that my eight-year-old daughter is really into fashion and she offered to give her a tour of her offices. I didn't expect that."

Roman had learned over time that people were just people. Heiress or not, Gracie was still a good person who cared deeply for others. "She is something special," he said. And he had to go in there and lie to her face. Because she was going to ask him about the Dax situation, and he had no information to give her.

"Hang on to that one," Mark said, opening the driver's side door.

He was trying. When he went back inside Gracie was clearing their plates from the table.

"Are you hungry?"

"I had a bite to eat at the office." The truth was he hadn't eaten all day. Not only did he have no appetite, but when he thought about lying to her he wanted to barf.

"Did you make any progress on those files?" she asked, putting the plates in the dishwasher.

Shit.

"I didn't," he said, which technically wasn't a lie. "But I put some feelers out and I'm waiting to hear from a few people."

Again, technically not a lie.

"Tonight I'd really just like to crash on the couch and watch TV."

"Sounds good," she said. "But first, can we talk about something?"

He had no idea what she wanted to talk about, but still his heart dropped. "Of course. What's up?"

"Roman," she said, walking over to him, tilting her chin up so she could look him in the eye. "There's something I have to say to you. Something I've wanted to say for a while now, but I… I just had to be sure."

"Okay," he said, heart in his throat, expecting the worst.

She cradled his face in her soft hands and looked him in the eye. "I forgive you."

A knife plunged through his heart couldn't have stung more, and though he was happy and relieved to hear the words, they were bittersweet. And he couldn't stop himself from what he said next. He took her hands and held them tight, looked deeply into her eyes and told her, "I love you, Gracie."

With misty eyes she smiled and said, "I love you, too," twisting the knife that much deeper.

He wrapped his arms around her, wishing he never had to let go again.

He had the love of his life back. He was finally right where he wanted to be. And now, due to circumstances completely out of his control, there was a pretty good chance that he could lose it all.

Gracie and Roman never did watch TV that night. They never even made it to the couch. They fell into bed together instead, and made love way past their bedtime. The way they had pretty much every night since.

In the following week Mark became a familiar fixture in her life. She hated that the driver had to be there, and as far as she knew there had been no nefarious activity, but if Roman thought it was necessary, she wasn't going to argue. But he hadn't made any headway to speak of on the files and she was getting impatient. If she didn't know better she might think he was stalling, but that ended tomorrow. She was going to ask him to bring the flash drive home so she could look at what was on it.

Home. That was an entirely new concept for her. When Roman gave her the all clear, would she be able to go back to her place? Would she be happy not seeing him every day, waking up to his smile and his messy hair? Would she feel alone without him to cuddle up to in bed? She had been at his place only a week yet somehow it felt like a lifetime.

And what if he asked her to stay? She'd been back to her place twice with Mark to pick up a few things. Well, more than a few actually. All of her makeup, hair products and toiletries were in Roman's bathroom. Half her wardrobe was hanging in the closet in the spare bedroom. Other than her furniture, she was practically moved in already. And it couldn't have felt more natural or more comfortable.

That didn't ease her nerves the day of her sister's wedding. This would be their first outing as a couple, and her entire family would be there. She thought her sisters would be okay; it was her mother and Sutton she was worried about. She wanted her sister's wedding to be perfect.

"I need help," Roman said, stepping into the bathroom, where she was putting the finishing touches on her makeup before she slipped into her gown.

He was dressed in his tux, and he looked so hot and sexy, she almost asked him to take it back off again. But they were already running late. They were supposed to be at Sutton's estate in less than an hour.

Roman held his bow tie out to her. "I've always sucked at these," he said, tugging at his collar. "I hate these damned monkey suits."

She tied a perfect knot, then stepped back to look at him. Perfect, other than the slightly rumpled hair. But that was just Roman. And it was getting long enough that he was due for a trim. She was so used to his hair that way, that when she saw photos of him with a military cut he was barely recognizable.

But still hot as hell.

"You look good," she said as he gave his collar another tug.

"Are you almost ready?" he asked her.

"Almost." She stepped over to the mirror and grabbed a bottle of hair spray, giving her updo another light misting. "Could you help me into my gown?"

Because the guest list was mostly family and good friends, she'd chosen to wear one of her own designs, a floor-length off-the-shoulder beaded dress the exact same color as her eyes. And it weighed a ton.

"What do you need me to do?" he asked.

"Zip me please." She pulled the dress down off the hanger and stepped into it. It took effort to get it up over her bosom and she knew that by the end of the night, lugging around the extra weight was going to wear on her.

He fastened the zipper and she turned to the mirror to see the final effect. Not half bad.

"You look beautiful," Roman said, stepping up behind her. He wrapped his arms around her middle and nibbled her shoulder. "Taste pretty good, too."

"And you smell delicious."

"Looking like you do, you might upstage the bride."

Not a chance. Having designed Nora's dress herself, Gracie knew her sister would be a knockout.

She turned in his arms and kissed him softly, so he didn't end up wearing more of her lipstick than she was. "I think I'm ready."

The way she was feeling right now, with so much happiness deep in her heart, she could take on the world.

Thirteen

By the time Gracie and Roman put on their coats and got into the limo her father had sent to fetch them, they were really late. It was windy and cold and lake-effect snow had begun to fall, making the surface roads slippery, adding more time to their drive.

When they finally made it to her father's estate the limo pulled up to the front steps and a valet opened the door.

They stepped into the foyer, which was a wonderland of draped pink and white tulle and a mix of pink and white blooms. In the foyer alone there had to be thousands of flowers, so she could only imagine how the rest of the house looked.

"Wow," Roman said under his breath. "That is a *lot* of pink."

She elbowed him playfully.

Her mother was the first person Gracie saw as she slipped out of her coat and handed it to an attendant.

Celeste saw them and eyed Roman coolly.

"So," Roman said. "She's clearly not happy to see me."

Gracie had wondered how she would take the news of her and Roman's reunion. Now she knew: not very well. "Give me a few minutes alone with her," Gracie said.

"Would you like a drink?" he asked.

"Not just yet. I need to pace myself."

"So, no more than four?" he teased.

She laughed. "Well, maybe five."

She crossed the foyer and Roman headed for the bar in the great room. Her mother opened her arms and gave Gracie a warm hug and an air-kiss. Celeste had always been beautiful, tall and lithe and graceful. But tonight she looked positively radiant.

"Mom, you look great!"

"I feel great," she said. "You look beautiful. Is the dress one of yours? It's lovely."

"It's mine. Have you seen Nora yet?"

"I was up there earlier for pictures. And Gracie, you've outdone yourself this time with her dress. It's absolutely stunning. And Eve's dress, oh my goodness. That's beautiful, too. Have I ever told you how talented you are, and how proud I am of you?"

"A time or two," Gracie said with a smile. Her mother had always been one of her biggest supporters. She'd raised her to be independent and think for herself. In part, Gracie guessed, because Celeste's parents had made most of her decisions for her. Like marrying Sutton.

"How was your trip?" Gracie asked.

Her mother lit up like a firefly. "Exactly what I needed."

"You look very happy."

With a coy smile, she said, "I have reason to be."

Could it be…? "Mom, did you meet someone?"

Her smile gave it away. "He's Italian. And ten years younger than me. And the sex?" She fanned her face and Gracie resisted the urge to put her fingers in her ears and sing, *la la la la la*. But she was so pleased to see her mother happy she didn't care. At sixty, Celeste was still young and vigorous.

Though her parents never had a great marriage, her mother had still taken the divorce and, more recently, the news of Carson's paternity hard. There was so much residual bitterness. Gracie had worried that being here would bring all of that hurt and turmoil back up to the surface on what should be a happy occasion.

"Your father doesn't look well at all," her mother commented. "It's obvious he hasn't much time left."

"I know," Gracie said, her heart aching a little at the thought of losing him. He wasn't a great *man*, but he had been a good father. It broke her heart to know that he wouldn't be there for her wedding, or to see his grandchildren if she had any. That was something she and Roman needed to talk about eventually. And speaking of… "So I guess you probably heard about me and Roman."

At the mention of his name, her mother's smile faded. "You know how I feel about him. About the hell that he put you through."

"I know, but I've forgiven him for that and we've moved forward." It had felt so good to say the words, to finally let go of the past and start fresh.

Her mother's lips dipped into a frown. "I don't trust him."

"But *I* do, and that's all that matters."

"You'll have to give me time to get used to this. Don't expect me to immediately welcome him with open arms just because you do."

The truth was, Gracie didn't really care what her mother or anyone else thought, because it wasn't their decision, or their business.

"I should probably go say hello to Daddy," she told her mother. "We'll talk more later."

"Of course," Celeste said, looking a little hurt. But Gracie was so happy and she didn't want anything to spoil her day.

As she walked through the house she saw so

many familiar faces. Though a Thanksgiving wedding was a little unconventional, everyone from the guest list seemed to be there. Carson and Georgia stood chatting with Gina Chamberlain, and Graham was at the bar with Roman. She had heard Brooks would not be attending, though out of courtesy he had been invited. Eve and Nash, as maid of honor and best man, were likely upstairs getting ready. But there were countless other friends and extended family, all of whom she would get to eventually, but as Nora had told her, she was a guest at this wedding. She would leave the formal greetings to the wedding party. This being her second marriage, Nora had chosen to keep it small and intimate. But Nora being Nora, she fretted over leaving her sister out. Gracie had been in the wedding party at Nora's first wedding, though. She just wanted her sister to do what made her happy.

After the ceremony in the arboretum, a sit-down turkey feast would be served in the ballroom, which hadn't been used in Grace couldn't remember how long, and there would be music and dancing afterward. When she was a child they used to have elaborate holiday celebrations with all of their friends and family, but as she and her sisters got older, and their parents' marriage got rockier, the parties had been few and far between.

She found her father sitting in his wheelchair,

nurse at the ready, amidst a group of business associates.

When he saw her approaching, he smiled. Despite her mother's observation, Gracie thought he looked pretty good today. He wasn't so pale, and he still looked dashing in a tux.

He shooed away the men and waved her closer.

"Princess, you look beautiful," he said as she leaned down to kiss his cheek.

"And you look handsome as usual."

"You know, after so many years of wearing a suit I actually miss my robe and slippers," he joked, and it was so nice to see him in good spirits. She'd been so busy at work lately she hadn't had much time to visit with him. She needed to make more of an effort.

"Are you still planning to walk Nora down the aisle?"

He nodded, a look of determination on his face. "If it kills me."

"Daddy, don't say that."

"I'm kidding. I'll be fine. I'm feeling good today."

She could see it, and she was so relieved. She had worried that he might be too ill to even attend. But he was tough, although much softer around the edges now and much more sentimental.

"Are you still at Roman's?" he asked her. The last time she'd seen her father she explained the entire situation, not sure if he would even remember the conversation. But apparently he had.

"I am. Until he thinks it's safe for me to go home."

"I never liked Dax," he said, frowning. "I never trusted him."

"I still can't believe I was so wrong about him. I feel so stupid."

"Don't," her father said, taking her hand. His felt cold and frail. "You see the good in people. It's your gift."

Some gift. In this instance it could have gotten her seriously hurt. Or possibly even killed.

For a fleeting second she thought about Roman, and how she had trusted him, too. But that was different.

Wasn't it?

A bell rang, alerting everyone that it was time to move to the arboretum for the ceremony. Nash appeared to wheel Sutton to the spot where he would meet Nora.

Roman stepped up beside Gracie and offered his arm, smiling so sweetly and looking so handsome she couldn't doubt him. She just needed to let it go and let herself be happy.

She took his arm and they found seats in the arboretum in the family section up near the front. A few minutes later Reid took his place beside the reverend, looking dashing in his tux and so happy. And maybe a little nervous, too. Nash stood beside him. Soft music played as Eve walked down the aisle, followed by Nash's niece, Phoebe, who sprinkled pink and white rose petals over the satin runner while her twin brother, Jude, watched anxiously from his mother's lap. Declan was next, looking adorable and debonair in his tux, carrying the pink pillow with the rings.

When the wedding march began everyone stood and turned, and when her sister appeared, Gracie's breath caught. In cream silk, with her pale complexion, Nora looked like a living porcelain statue. Her dress was simple but elegant and fit her perfectly. Gracie couldn't help but give herself a pat on the back.

"You've outdone yourself," Roman said softly, making her smile.

Sutton moved slowly, bracing himself against his daughter, but held his head high. And when he gave her away to Reid Gracie could swear there were tears in his eyes.

The ceremony was short but heartfelt, and when Declan got restless and wanted Mommy, Nora and Reid held him together as they spoke their vows. And when they kissed, he kissed them, too. It was probably the sweetest thing that Gracie had ever seen. They were truly a family united by love, and for a moment Grace wanted that so badly for herself it almost hurt. That would be her and Roman someday. Getting married, having a family. Growing old together. She knew it beyond a shadow of doubt.

The reception afterward truly was a feast, but the guilt chewing a hole in Roman's gut made it almost impossible to eat. He found himself wishing there was a family dog he could slip his dinner to, the way he had when he was a kid. When Gracie asked him if something was wrong, he told her the whiskey he'd drunk earlier had upset his stomach. Her look of sympathy, and her offer to go find him an antacid, nearly did him in.

He would drink himself into a stupor if he thought it would help, but he'd never been one to use alcohol as a crutch. He knew too many soldiers who turned to drinking to deal with their PTSD and he refused to go there. But at times like this it was tempting.

After dinner they mingled, but Roman noticed that Sutton, back in his wheelchair, didn't look so good. Maybe a little bit of Grace was rubbing off on Roman. He could hardly believe he had sympathy for the man, considering what a son of a bitch he'd always been. Sitting alone with his nurse at his side, Sutton looked so old and frail and sullen. He was too weak to even dance with Nora. And Roman felt compelled to do something.

What the hell.

Roman walked over to Sutton, nudged his nurse aside and said, "You look like you need a breather."

The relief was clear on Sutton's face. "My suite," he said, so Roman pushed him there, and strangely enough no one seemed to notice or care. The shark was gone, reduced to nothing more than…a goldfish. A sick, helpless old man. But Roman knew that he would never be forgotten. He'd made his mark on the world, and no one could ever take that from him. But clearly he was ready to throw in the towel. Ready to let someone take over his legacy. He had groomed Eve to be the shark that he'd once been, but with her softer side, she would rule the family business with compassion and heart. And she would never have to live with the regret that was so obvious in Sutton's expression. He'd lived large and fast, and burned out before his time. Roman hoped that if nothing else, Sutton's children had learned from his mistakes.

Sutton ordered his nurse to take her seat in the hallway, and when the door was closed and they were alone, he told Roman, "Thank you."

"Don't thank me. I needed a breather, too," he said, brushing his thanks off, realizing that it was actually disturbing to see such a powerful man reduced to this. What a terrible way to go.

"Help me into bed?" Sutton asked, surprising Roman again.

Without a word Roman helped him undress and change into his pajamas. He was too weak to stand so Roman literally had to lift him into his bed.

"I'm tired, Roman," he said, as he settled back against the pillows. "I'm tired of fighting."

"I understand," Roman said, and he did. There were times, as a POW, when he'd been tempted to give up, to let the enemy win, but he'd kept on fighting. But his enemy had been radical Al Qaeda soldiers. Sutton's enemy was cancer, and it was eating him from the inside out.

"I know you do," Sutton said, then asked, "Have you heard from Agent Crosswell?"

Roman was stunned into silence, and Sutton just smiled. "I may be a sick old man, but I still have connections. After what Dax Caufield did to my daughter…" He shook his head and frowned, as if he couldn't bear to think about it. "I knew he was crooked, but I also knew that eventually he would be exposed for who he really was. I never thought he was dangerous. Especially not to Grace. When I heard what happened I took matters into my own hands and made a few calls."

"No, I haven't heard from him," Roman said. "But I'm hoping to soon."

"You love my daughter."

The question caught him off guard. "Yes, I do." He always had.

"And I trust that you'll keep her safe."

"I lied to her," he said, the words coming out of nowhere. "I lied to her again."

He expected Sutton to be angry, but instead he said, "Yes. But you did it to keep her safe."

That didn't make it right. "She may not see it that way."

"Roman," he said. "I love all of my children equally. I may not show it, but I do. But Grace? There's something special about her. She always sees the good in people. She always gives people the benefit of the doubt. God knows she's done it for me. She will forgive you."

Roman wasn't so sure. "I lied to her."

"You didn't have a choice."

No, but that still didn't make it right. "I have to tell her the truth."

"You will, when the time is right. And she'll forgive you, and give you another chance. Because that's who she is."

Again, Roman wasn't so sure about that.

"When you get home tonight, turn on the news."

Sutton obviously knew something he didn't. "Why?"

The old man's smile was devious, and for an instant he looked like the Sutton he used to be. "As I said, I still have my connections."

Without elaborating, Sutton closed his eyes, and in an instant he was asleep, leaving Roman to wonder if they had arrested Dax today, or were planning to.

He left Sutton sleeping and headed back to the

ballroom, but Carson, on his way to the den, told him, "Roman, you have to see this."

Roman followed him, joining a large group of the wedding guests gathered around the television. It was tuned to the news, and the banner across the screen screamed State Senator Arrested on Fraud Charges.

And sure enough, there was Dax on the screen being led away from his home in handcuffs. The relief Roman felt left him weak. He could finally talk to Gracie and tell her the truth. And he could stop worrying about her safety.

He saw Gracie standing over by the bar, a drink in her hand, and she waved him over.

"Is this really happening?" she said, looking dazed.

"It's really happening." And it was about time.

"I knew something was up, but I never expected this."

Clearly no one had if the shocked expressions and low hum of incredulous chatter were any indication.

"Does this mean I'm safe now?" she asked Roman, looking so hopeful it made him feel about an inch tall.

"I hope so." Things would be dicey, and he was sure that she would be getting a visit from the FBI. Which meant he had to tell her the truth, before she heard it from someone else. So he said, "We need to talk."

She frowned. "Right now?"

"Yes, right now."

Fourteen

Something in Roman's voice, in his troubled expression, put her instantly on edge. Shouldn't he be happy that this mess was finally going to be over and she could get her life back? And why did she get the feeling that he knew something she didn't?

"We can go to my room," she said. Like her sisters she still kept a room at the estate, so she led Roman there.

When they were inside with the door closed, she asked him, "What's going on? I couldn't help but notice that you didn't seem at all surprised by the news report. Or relieved."

"I knew this was coming," he said. "I just didn't know when."

A feeling of dread started in her heart and trickled downward into her belly. "How did you know?"

He sat on the edge of the bed, wearing a look of pure misery, which only made her feel worse.

"I've been working with the FBI," he said.

And he hadn't told her. Her heart started to thump. "How long?"

"They contacted me the day before Dax came to your place. They knew that he wanted the backup flash drive, and they wanted to get their hands on it first."

She closed her eyes and took a deep breath. Oh no he didn't. He couldn't have. "You found something, didn't you? In the files that first night."

Eyes lowered, he nodded.

"So you lied to me."

He nodded again.

She felt eerily calm as she asked him, "And where is the flash drive now?"

"I turned it over to the FBI last week."

So he hadn't really been going through the files looking for evidence. That was just another lie.

He could not be doing this to her again. Not now. Not after she had forgiven him, and given him her heart. He just couldn't.

The dread grew exponentially, sucking her into a place so dark and foreboding she wanted to disappear.

"They didn't give me a choice. You were going to be implicated in the case. I gave them the flash drive in exchange for your immunity."

She blinked, then blinked again. "Because you thought I was guilty."

His head shot up. "No! To protect you."

"Why would you have to protect me, and make a deal for me, if you knew I hadn't done anything wrong?"

"Gracie," he said, reaching for her.

She stepped back, repulsed by the thought of his hands on her. It was seven years ago happening all over again. "Don't touch me."

"It wasn't like that," he said, standing. "You have to believe me. I was just trying to keep you safe."

"I don't," she said, aware that she had started to tremble. "I don't believe you. And I don't trust you. I won't trust you ever again."

"If you'll let me explain—"

She had only seen him look this crushed once before: the last time he'd betrayed her. "No. There's no excuse you could give me that would justify you lying to me. You doubted me. Again. I'm finished."

"Gracie, please—" He reached for her again, touched her arm and she ripped it away.

"Get out," she said.

She could feel it coming on, the total collapse of her soul. She was crumbling from the inside out.

She wanted to scream at him, and pound his chest with her fists, make him *feel* how much he'd hurt her. But at this point why bother? It was over. For good. And with that realization, the last of her will fizzled away. She just wanted to hide. She was so cold and empty she just wanted to curl up in bed, close her eyes and sleep until the ache in her heart went away. But she had the feeling that this time his deceit ran so deep, the pain would never go away. This was her so-called "gift" of seeing the best in everyone biting her in the ass again. She'd believed in Roman when he said he loved her, and had given him the benefit of the doubt when deep down she'd felt as if something wasn't right. And once again she'd been burned.

"Gracie, please talk to me," he said.

She shook her head. There was nothing to talk about. It was over. "Roman," she said, her voice eerily calm, "I want you to leave, and I never want to see you again."

Unable to even look at him any longer, she crossed the room and stepped into the bathroom, shutting the door and leaning against it, her heart pounding so hard and fast she felt light-headed and sick. So sick that she dashed to the commode, barely making it in time before she lost her dinner.

She sat on the floor, still in her gown, waiting for the tears to come, but she was so dead inside she just felt numb. The perpetual optimism was gone, and in its place something dark and cold took over, making her determined to hold on to and protect her heart, and never let another man hurt her again.

Gracie had an amazing dream. It was her and Roman's wedding, and they were so happy and in love, but as she slowly woke and opened her eyes and realized where she was, the memory of last night came rushing back with an intensity that made it hard to breathe. She couldn't even scrape together the will to lift her head. She'd been depressed before, but right now she felt utterly destroyed. And that was when the tears started, and they didn't stop again for three days. She spent the entire holiday weekend in bed, sleeping, crying and hating herself for trusting him. She couldn't eat, couldn't concentrate and on Monday when she should have gone back to work, she called in sick.

When she finally worked up the will to get out of bed and charge her long-dead cell phone, she was bombarded by dozens of text messages and voice mails. But none from Roman, which made her feel both relieved and heartsick. An Agent Crosswell from the FBI and a federal prosecutor had left several messages. As a player in Dax's campaign, of course she would be questioned and probably asked to testify. Just one more mess brought on by her "gift." Or her curse as she'd now begun to see it.

Tuesday she finally ventured downstairs to the kitchen for a bite to eat, barely able to choke down a bagel with cream cheese. The wedding decor had been replaced with holiday decorations that would be up till the first of the new year. But she couldn't enjoy it.

She was headed back upstairs, when she passed her father's nurse, who looked surprised to see her.

"Miss Winchester, I didn't know you were here."

"How is my father?" She'd been so wrapped up in her own problems she hadn't even thought to check up on him.

"The wedding took a lot out of him. He's mostly been sleeping. He feels better today, though."

"I should probably go say hello."

"I'm sure he would like that. Your visits always cheer him up."

"Take a break and I'll sit with him awhile," Gracie said.

With a frown, the woman asked her, "Are you okay?"

She must have looked absolutely awful. She hadn't eaten or showered in days. She hadn't even looked in the mirror. She was too ashamed to face her own reflection.

"I'm fine."

"There have been a lot of calls since Thursday. Mostly from reporters."

Well, that was no big surprise. They had been

calling her, too. But she didn't want to talk about it, or even think about it. "Thank you for the warning. I'll call if I need you."

She went to her father's suite, knocking lightly before opening the door and peeking inside. He was sitting propped up in bed working on his laptop. When he saw her, he smiled. "Princess, I didn't know you were visiting today."

He obviously had no idea that she'd never left. And as she drew closer to his bed, his smile began to fade. "Princess, what's wrong?"

With an ache that was all consuming, she sat beside him, laid her head in his lap and cried while her father stroked her hair. And it was exactly what she needed.

When she was all out of tears, he handed her a tissue and she wiped her eyes. "I suppose you probably heard what happened," she said. "How stupid I've been. How he betrayed me again. I should have listened to you. I should have trusted you when you said he was no good for me."

"But you went with your heart instead."

She nodded. "You must be pretty happy that it's over."

"On the contrary. I think you're making the biggest mistake in your life."

His words took her aback. "But…"

"Be quiet and listen. Do you know why I insisted

you attend that initial meeting with Roman, and why I asked you to get close to him?"

"To avoid another scandal."

"There wasn't going to be another scandal. I knew that Brooks was working alone to discredit me in the media, and that Roman had no part in his twisted revenge plot."

Gracie frowned. "I don't understand. Why did you make me do it, then? Were you trying to torture me?"

"I was trying to make you see what I've seen all along. That you still loved him."

What? "But…you don't even like him. You never did. You always tried to come between us."

"I was jealous."

His words stunned her. "Jealous? Of what?"

"Princess, since the day you were born, you were a daddy's girl. You wouldn't go to sleep at night if I wasn't there to tuck you in. Despite all of the horrible things in my life you still saw the good in me. I didn't want to lose you to someone else."

Is that how he really felt? Did he really love her that much? She could hardly imagine him so vulnerable. "Daddy, you could never lose me. You're my father. I'll always love you."

"I didn't see it that way. And I was wrong." He took her hands in his. "I don't want you to make the same mistake that I did. I let the love of my life go, and I never stopped regretting it."

She didn't have to ask who. She'd heard the rumors. "Cynthia Newport."

He nodded, looking so sad. "I tried to fill the void, but I was never able to let her go. Learn from my mistakes. Don't do that to yourself. Talk to Roman. He loves you."

Her father didn't understand. "He lied to me. That's not love."

"He was protecting you."

"He thought I was guilty."

"No, he was fighting to prove that you weren't. You have no idea what you got yourself into. As a part of Dax's campaign, you were implicated in the fraud. You could have been prosecuted. Roman made a deal with the FBI. Your flash drive in exchange for full immunity."

"So why didn't he just tell me the truth? When the FBI called, why didn't he tell me?"

"He couldn't."

"He didn't trust me."

"It wasn't about trust. He was under the thumb of the FBI. What they did was nothing shy of blackmail. He couldn't tell you, and if he did you could have both been prosecuted. He couldn't take that chance."

Through the darkness in her soul a dim shimmer of light appeared. She thought about the way Roman had taken care of her and protected her when he thought her life was in danger.

"He loves you, Princess. Don't you see that? He did what he had to, knowing that when he told you the truth he could lose you forever. But it was a chance he had to take. He loved you so much, and wanted you to be safe, so he took the gamble."

And lost. But she hadn't even let him explain. She had been so wrapped up in her own pain she couldn't even make herself listen.

The dim light grew a little brighter. "How do you know all of this?"

"He confided in me Thursday night."

She blinked. Roman had confided in Sutton? His mortal enemy? It was almost too far-fetched to believe. And if he really had done it just to protect her…

Once again, a flicker of hope broke through the gloom. Was it possible that this wasn't really the end? Shouldn't she at least give him a chance to explain?

He squeezed her hand. "Talk to him, Grace."

She had been pretty awful to him Thursday night. "What if he doesn't want to talk to me?"

"He does."

"How do you know?"

"I just do. I know that over the years I've expected a lot from you, and I'm asking you now, for the last time, to do one more thing for me."

"What, Daddy?"

"I'm asking you to trust me."

When he said it like that, with so much love in his eyes, how could she tell him no?

Fifteen

For five days following the wedding, Roman barely existed, trapped in his own personal hell. The hell he had created. Again. He hadn't eaten or slept. He hadn't been back to work. He'd basically wandered around the house in a daze, trying to figure out a way to fix this, and coming up with nothing.

Sutton had been wrong about her forgiving him. And as every new day passed, he knew it was less and less likely that he would ever hear from her again. In his efforts to protect Gracie he'd hurt her so deeply that she had completely shut him out.

It hadn't been the first time, but it would definitely be the last. She was clearly done with him.

She wouldn't even let him explain, and he didn't blame her. Why would she?

He needed to pack her things so he could send them to her, but he hadn't been able to make himself do it. Everything was exactly as she'd left it, and there wasn't a square inch of his home that didn't remind him of her. It didn't even feel like home anymore. Not without her there. She'd left her mark indelibly on his entire world. He would have to sell his house and move if he was ever going to have a chance of forgetting her. But he doubted even that would work.

But at least she was safe, and protected from prosecution. At least he had given her that. And she would never know how much, and for how long, he had loved her. It hadn't even been clear to him until he lost her.

Around two his doorbell rang, and for a second he felt an actual sliver of hope that it might be her, but that was just him living in a fantasy world. She was gone. Out of his life. And the sooner he accepted that the better off he would be.

But when he opened the door, he was sure that he was hallucinating from lack of sleep, because that couldn't possibly be Gracie standing there on his porch. She looked up at him, her face expressionless, as if she were waiting for him to say something.

All he could come up with was "Back for your things?"

Without warning she launched herself at him so forcefully he stumbled backward, and when she wrapped her arms around him, Roman was so stunned that for a second he didn't even hug her back.

Now he knew he had to be hallucinating. But when he pulled her close to him, she couldn't have felt more real. He buried his face in the softness of her hair and breathed her in.

Yep, she was definitely there. The question was why.

"I'm sorry," she said, holding on tight. "I'm so sorry."

Wait. What?

She was sorry? That made no sense. He must have misheard.

He peeled her away from him and held her at arm's length, managing a dumbfounded-sounding "What?"

"I said I'm sorry."

Was this some kind of sick joke she was playing on him? "What could you possibly have done to be sorry for? I'm the one who's sorry. I lied to you."

"And I loved you, and that I trusted you, then I didn't even give you a chance to explain. I was so angry and so hurt that all I cared about was protecting myself. I didn't even think about you and how hard it must have been keeping that from me. And the risk you took to keep me safe."

He wanted to pinch himself to make sure that he was actually awake.

"I wish I could take credit for realizing what I was doing, but it took a talking-to from my father to open my eyes."

Wait a minute…it was Sutton who'd saved his ass?

Looking crushed, she said, "I let you down and I'm sorry."

"You think you let me down?" he asked incredulously. Maybe *she* was the one hallucinating. "*I* let *you* down."

She shook her head. "No, you didn't. You probably saved my life. I was just too stupid to see it. But I see it now, and I'm begging you to give me another chance."

She was the one begging? "Gracie, I should be begging you. And I would have, but I didn't think… I just assumed you would never want to speak to me again."

"Like the last time," she said, and he nodded. "This is different. I know that, deep in my soul. You're my forever. My home."

He cradled her face in his hands and kissed her softly. "And you're mine. You always have been."

She gazed up at him with a smile. "So does that mean you'll give me a second chance?"

"Yes, of course I will," he said, pulling her into his arms. And a third and a fourth and a fifth chance. Anything to keep her in his life, because she was his everything. "I want to spend the rest of my life with you. I want to marry you, and have a family with you. It's what I've always wanted."

"Me, too," she said. "And if that's a proposal my answer is yes."

He grinned. "Sweetheart, when I formally propose you'll know it. I'm pulling out all the stops. I want to do this right."

She deserved the best, and that's what he would give her. And though he'd thought for sure that he'd ruined it, she was giving him another chance, too. A second chance at the love of a lifetime.

* * * * *

Don't miss a single installment of
DYNASTIES: THE NEWPORTS

*Passion and chaos consume
a Chicago real estate empire*

SAYING YES TO THE BOSS
by Andrea Laurence

AN HEIR FOR THE BILLIONAIRE
by Kat Cantrell

CLAIMED BY THE COWBOY
by Sarah M. Anderson

HIS SECRET BABY BOMBSHELL
by Jules Bennett

BACK IN THE ENEMY'S BED
by Michelle Celmer

Available now from Harlequin Desire!

And

THE TEXAN'S ONE NIGHT STAND-OFF
by Charlene Sands

Available December 2016!

***

*If you're on Twitter, tell us what you think
of Harlequin Desire! #harlequindesire*

COMING NEXT MONTH FROM

HARLEQUIN
Desire

Available December 6, 2016

#2485 THE BABY PROPOSAL
Billionaires and Babies • by Andrea Laurence
Lana will do anything to gain custody of her infant niece—even marry her best friend, Kal, in name only. But playing house in Kal's mansion has them both wanting to be much more than friends...

#2486 THE TEXAN'S ONE-NIGHT STANDOFF
Dynasties: The Newports • by Charlene Sands
Brooks Newport's scorching one-night stand with Ruby Lopez was unforgettable—and he wants more! Until a reunion with his long-lost father reveals Ruby to be an honorary member of the family...and completely off-limits.

#2487 MAID UNDER THE MISTLETOE
by Maureen Child
After a tragic past, millionaire Sam Henry enjoys being alone, especially for Christmas. But will his temporary holiday housekeeper's sexy smiles and enticing touch lure him back into the world—and tempt him to take a second chance on love?

#2488 THE PREGNANCY PROJECT
Love and Lipstick • by Kat Cantrell
Dante has made a fortune as Dr. Sexy. So he knows attraction when he feels it—even when the temptation is his pregnant best friend who's sworn off men! Now this expert at seduction must prove his theories work—while holding on to his heart.

#2489 RICH RANCHER FOR CHRISTMAS
The Beaumont Heirs • by Sarah M. Anderson
CJ Wesley is a Beaumont heir, and that's a secret he won't share. Especially not with a sexy-as-sin city girl looking for her next big story. But when a snowstorm strands these opposites on his ranch, their white-hot attraction proves impossible to resist!

#2490 MARRIED TO THE MAVERICK MILLIONAIRE
From Mavericks to Married • by Joss Wood
Millionaire hockey star Quinn agrees to a marriage of convenience to avoid scandal and save the biggest deal of his career. But an unplanned kiss at a masked ball ignites a fiery attraction to his new wife he can't ignore...

YOU CAN FIND MORE INFORMATION ON UPCOMING HARLEQUIN® TITLES, FREE EXCERPTS AND MORE AT WWW.HARLEQUIN.COM.

HDCNM1116

REQUEST YOUR FREE BOOKS!
2 FREE NOVELS PLUS 2 FREE GIFTS!

H HARLEQUIN®

Desire

ALWAYS POWERFUL, PASSIONATE AND PROVOCATIVE

YES! Please send me 2 FREE Harlequin® Desire novels and my 2 FREE gifts (gifts are worth about $10). After receiving them, if I don't wish to receive any more books, I can return the shipping statement marked "cancel." If I don't cancel, I will receive 6 brand-new novels every month and be billed just $4.55 per book in the U.S. or $5.24 per book in Canada. That's a savings of at least 13% off the cover price! It's quite a bargain! Shipping and handling is just 50¢ per book in the U.S. and 75¢ per book in Canada.* I understand that accepting the 2 free books and gifts places me under no obligation to buy anything. I can always return a shipment and cancel at any time. Even if I never buy another book, the two free books and gifts are mine to keep forever.

225/326 HDN GH2P

Name _____ (PLEASE PRINT) _____

Address _____ Apt. # _____

City _____ State/Prov. _____ Zip/Postal Code _____

Signature (if under 18, a parent or guardian must sign)

Mail to the **Reader Service:**

IN U.S.A.: P.O. Box 1867, Buffalo, NY 14240-1867
IN CANADA: P.O. Box 609, Fort Erie, Ontario L2A 5X3

Want to try two free books from another line?
Call 1-800-873-8635 or visit www.ReaderService.com.

* Terms and prices subject to change without notice. Prices do not include applicable taxes. Sales tax applicable in N.Y. Canadian residents will be charged applicable taxes. Offer not valid in Quebec. This offer is limited to one order per household. Not valid for current subscribers to Harlequin Desire books. All orders subject to credit approval. Credit or debit balances in a customer's account(s) may be offset by any other outstanding balance owed by or to the customer. Please allow 4 to 6 weeks for delivery. Offer available while quantities last.

Your Privacy—The Reader Service is committed to protecting your privacy. Our Privacy Policy is available online at www.ReaderService.com or upon request from the Reader Service.

We make a portion of our mailing list available to reputable third parties that offer products we believe may interest you. If you prefer that we not exchange your name with third parties, or if you wish to clarify or modify your communication preferences, please visit us at www.ReaderService.com/consumerchoice or write to us at Reader Service Preference Service, P.O. Box 9062, Buffalo, NY 14240-9062. Include your complete name and address.

HD15

"What about moving in with me?"

Lana looked at him, narrowing her eyes. "That would help a lot, actually. Are you sure, though? It's going to be a major cramp on your bachelorhood to have me and a baby in the house."

Kal shrugged that off. He rarely had time for anything aside from work this time of year. Plus, if Lana was in the house with the baby, he wouldn't miss out on his time with her. He'd never admit to his selfish motivations, however. "I've got three extra bedrooms just sitting empty. If it will help, I'm happy to do what I can."

Lana beamed at him. "I'm actually really glad you said that, because I was just about to get to the crazy part of my plan."

Kal swallowed hard. She had something in mind that was crazier than moving in together with a baby?

Just then Lana slid off her chair and onto one knee in

front of him. She took his hand and held it as he frowned down at her. "What are you doing?" he asked as his chest grew tight and he struggled to breathe. His hand was suddenly burning up where she held it in hers, the contact lighting his every nerve on fire. He wanted to pull away and regain control of himself, but he knew he couldn't. This was just the calm before the storm.

Lana took a deep breath and looked up at him with a hopeful smile. "I'm asking you to marry me."

Don't miss
THE BABY PROPOSAL
by Andrea Laurence,
available December 2016 wherever
Harlequin® Desire books and ebooks are sold.

www.Harlequin.com

Whatever You're Into... Passionate Reads

Looking for more passionate reads from Harlequin®?
Fear not! Harlequin® Presents, Harlequin® Desire and
Harlequin® Blaze offer you irresistible romance stories
featuring powerful heroes.

⬥HARLEQUIN® *Presents.*

Do you want alpha males, decadent glamour and jet-set
lifestyles? Step into the sensational, sophisticated world of
Harlequin® Presents, where sinfully tempting heroes ignite a
fierce and wickedly irresistible passion!

⬥HARLEQUIN® *Desire*

Harlequin® Desire novels are powerful, passionate and
provocative contemporary romances set against a backdrop of
wealth, privilege and sweeping family saga. Alpha heroes with
a soft side meet strong-willed but vulnerable heroines amid a
dramatic world of divided loyalties, high-stakes conflict and
intense emotion.

⬥HARLEQUIN® *Blaze*

Harlequin® Blaze stories sizzle with strong heroines and
irresistible heroes playing the game of modern love and lust.
They're fun, sexy and always steamy.

Be sure to check out our full selection of books
within each series every month!